Front cover shows *Poppies*
inspired by the poem *In Flan*
The stained glass panel was
artists and poets who f
<u>www.rachelmulligan.co.uk</u>

This book is dedicated to the

Royal Army Medical Corps

Second Edition (2019)

First Edition Printed December 2018

Contents

LEONARD FOLWELL

LEONARD'S FAMILY

Ernest, Leonard, May, Stanley and Beatrice

"Leonard's War"

What has been really interesting for me was writing this story one hundred years after World War 1.

I was inspired to write this story when I learnt that York Railway Museum was putting on an exhibition about WW1 Ambulance Trains.

I had my grandfather's diary from WW1 so decided I really ought to copy it onto the computer. It took several months to copy the fine italic pencil writing out by hand and then onto the computer. By the time the exhibition had started I had a copy for the museum to keep.

We were invited up to the York Railway Museum for the open evening. There we met other people who had had relatives who had worked on the Ambulance Trains during WW1.

There was a plaque in remembrance of the people who had worked on the Ambulance Trains and half way down the list was 'Leonard Folwell.'

My husband also bought me the book "All I Have to Give" by Mary Wood, the well-known author. It was a story based around WW1. At the end of the story I was interested to learn that Mary and her husband Roy had been to France and had travelled around the towns and villages that were involved in the First World War.

I contacted Mary as a lot of the towns and villages were also mentioned in my grandfather's diary.

Mary and I became friends and her continued support, despite being very busy with her own work, has been extremely helpful.

I would like to thank my husband Chris for his continuous support also my neighbour Kay for her help with putting the story together and correcting my spelling mistakes. Also thank you to Bill who read through the story. Thank you to Colin for the drawing of the Zeppelin. Thank you to Alison French for your help putting the book on Amazon.

My husband Chris and I went on a cruise in 2016. We went from Southampton across to Le Havre where we went up the River Seine to Rouen, exactly 100 years since my grandfather did.

Chapter One

<u>Tragedy on the Home Front</u>

Ernest Folwell stood up and stretched. He had sat in this crouched position for most of the afternoon. He tidied the tools on his bench into a neat line, untied his leather apron and hung it on a hook by the door. As Ernest looked around the old premises that he had inherited from his father, he noticed how dingy it looked in the late afternoon light. It needed a lick of paint to brighten the place up a bit. He knew there was a war going on and business had not been too good of late but if he and his son, Leonard, spent a morning washing down walls and painting the woodwork, it would make all the difference.

'That's enough for today, lad!' he said to Leonard.

Leonard looked up from his work. Was it that time already? Leonard was of smaller stature than his father. He had dark hair, deep-set eyes and bushy eyebrows, all set in a weathered rustic complexion.

They left the shop together and headed for the railway station. The streets of Leicester were busy, but neither noticed. They looked like twins with the same swarthy looks, both wearing black overcoats and matching bowler hats.

Ernest stopped, as he always did, at the newspaper stand. He sorted out some loose change from his deep pocket. The vendor folded the paper neatly and handed it to Ernest, then doffed his cap.

'Good evening, gents. Mind how you go.'

Ernest, a thoughtful man of few words, smiled in response. Like his work bench, he was neat and tidy. His hair was brushed to one side; he had a moustache, was tall and good-looking. He put the folded newspaper into his brief case, but not before he caught sight of the bill board:

"The Quintinshill Rail Disaster*!*** *Tragedy on the Home Front."*

It's bad enough there's a war going on and our troops are being killed in France and Belgium without losing forces on our home turf, he thought to himself,

As they neared the railway station, Leonard noticed a queue of men, some no more than lads, waiting to join the army. A sergeant in full uniform stood at a tall desk with leaflets and papers. He was talking to the men and boys, and they were signing a paper and being given a 'King's Shilling'. Leonard noticed how most of the men walked away very pleased with themselves, laughing and patting each other on the back.

As they boarded the train was rather busy but both men found a seat and sat quietly on the journey home, both deep in thought. Ernest ruminated on the news headline he had just read, and Leonard remembered the look on the men's faces as they left the stand after signing up.

It took only half an hour to travel from Leicester to Woodhouse Eaves.   Theirs was the first stop, so the train was still fairly crowded. They walked the short distance home. Dinner smelled good as they opened the back door and the warmth from within hit them.

Beatrice had been busy cooking a stew all afternoon, adding vegetables from the garden to make it go further. She had also cooked potatoes in their jackets to serve with the stew and a creamy rice pudding for afters.

Beatrice was an attractive lady with long, rather wispy hair that she tried to tie up in a bun. The feathery strands added to her attraction. She had a beautiful complexion for her age and soft blue eyes behind auburn eye lashes. Ernest kissed her lightly on the cheek.

'I've lit the fire in the room. Dinner won't be too long. I'll bring you both a cup of tea in a minute.'

After dinner, Ernest took out his newspaper and read the dreadful story of the train crash that had taken place in Scotland. A train had been stationary on the main railway line when the train carrying 400 Soldiers from the 7th Scottish Regiment crashed into it at full speed with no warning. The old wooden coaches had been taken from disused stock and should never have been used in the first place. Lit by gas lamps, the gas cylinders had burst on impact, setting the coaches on fire like a tinder box. To make matters worse, within two minutes an express overnight train travelling from Euston to Scotland then crashed into the wreckage.

A burning inferno had followed resulting in 230 dead and 246 injured. The Scottish Regiment had been on their way to Liverpool, ready to sail across and join the fighting in Gallipoli.

Ernest folded his paper and headed outside to smoke his pipe.

'Are you alright, love?' asked Beatrice. 'You're quieter than usual.'

'Yes, love. It's been a long day and I feel very tired tonight.' Ernest didn't want to worry his pretty wife; she did a good job looking after the family of five. She was worried about the war and she would find out sooner or later about this dreadful tragedy.

Ernest stood outside watching the mist descend over the field. A weak moon shone through casting ghostly shadows and an owl hooted in the distant wood. He shivered as he made his way indoors.

That night Leonard took the newspaper upstairs and read of the day's awful news by the candlelight in his bedroom. It affected him more than he would have hoped. He spent a restless night.

The next morning, at work in their shop making and mending shoes, Leonard turned to his father and said, 'Terrible job, those Scottish troops being killed like that. It really upset me.'

'Yes it was,' answered his father.

'I feel that maybe I should help towards the war effort. So I'm … I'm thinking of signing up, Father. What do you think?'

Ernest slowly put his tools down to listen to what his son had to say.

'I think it would be best if I joined the Army.' Leonard felt uncomfortable with the pause.

'Well, lad,' said Ernest slowly,' you're of an age where you can make up your own mind. But yes, I think you would make a fine solider. Your mother won't be too keen on the idea. You know how she worries and, of course, you are her first born and a son to be proud of.'

'I know. I don't want to upset mother, but she still has our May and Stanley at home, and I need to fly the nest sometime. This seems like an ideal time to me. I do hope she understands. Perhaps you could have a word with her for me?'

'Yes, lad, I'll do that for you. If you believe you have a calling to join the army then that is what you must do. I think your mother will get used to the idea, given time.'

Both men spent the next hour mending the few shoes that had been brought in. Leonard had ordered some softer leather so he could start making men's wallets and ladies' purses. One of his best sellers was a man's belt with a concealed wallet sewn into the back.

That weekend, Leonard went round to call for his friend John. They had been best friends since they started school together. It was John who had shortened Leonard to Len and it had stuck. Leonard's mother was not over keen but Leonard liked it.

John was a quiet lad and quite shy. He was not as tall as Leonard and had curly ginger hair. His teenage years had not been good to him. He had suffered terrible acne and his skin was pock marked with scar tissue, which did nothing for his confidence.

Len knocked on the back door and John's mother opened it.

'Hello, Mrs Hill. Is your John about?' asked Len politely.

'Come on in, lad, he's just helping me with the washing up. Would you like a cuppa?'

'Yes please, if you're making one!'

The three of them sat at the kitchen table and talked about the sinking of the Lusitania.

'Yes it was dreadful. There were a lot of families on the ship, women and children,' said John. 'It was hit by a German U-Boat. It had travelled from America heading to Liverpool and was torpedoed not far from the coast of southern Ireland.'

'Yes, I heard the Germans believed it was carrying weapons for the war effort.' said Len.

'It reminds me of the sinking of the Titanic. Too few lifeboats. Can you imagine the sheer blind panic on board?'

'Yes, we have a lot to be thankful for in Woodhouse Eaves,' replied John's mother.

'Right, let me get me cap and jacket. See you later, Mum,' John shouted as he closed the door.

'You alright, mate?' asked John as he looked again at Len's pale face.

'Yes. I'm okay.'

The two pals headed towards their favourite walk - up past the church with its square tower and stained glass window facing east to catch the early morning sun. They passed the Manor House with its Jacobean double front and heavily leaded windows. Over the style then down towards the river. An old rope used by the boys in their younger days as a swing hung lifeless from a branch.

The river ran fast after last night's rain.

'Did you hear about that terrible train crash in this week's newspaper?' asked a worried Len.

'Yes, they were talking about it yesterday at work. Terrible business!'

'John, it's got me thinking of signing up for the army. Have you thought of signing up? We could join together,' said Len.

'I know I should, Len, but I'm afraid,' said John, as he kicked a sod of earth across the grass.

'But look at that story in this week's newspaper. You could die like they did in a train crash, or be knocked over by a bus. None of us are immortal. '

'I'm not sure. I don't feel as brave as you are. If I could stay with you, Len, I would probably be okay, but you know how I worry so,' replied John

'Well, the best thing to do is go into Leicester to the recruitment office one day this week and see what we can sort out. Let's go in on Tuesday morning. That gives us time to have a word with our parents. I'm pretty sure mine will be alright, but you are the only one, John, and I'm sure your mother will need some time to adjust to the situation. I shall join anyway, but I don't want to force you into anything.'

So it was that, ten days later, Len and John found themselves in the queue outside the recruitment office. Two posters depicted Lord Kitchener pointing the forefinger of his large hand as he stared stony faced, at the waiting men.

 'Your Country Needs You!' was emblazoned below his face in large black letters.

Lord Kitchener had a long military background and had predicted that the war would be a lengthy affair. He had been recalled to England from Cairo the day before war was declared, and had been made Secretary of State for War by the Prime Minister, Herbert Asquith. Lord Kitchener encouraged men in their thousands to join up. He promised young men who were at university that they could continue their studies at the end of the war.

He encouraged lads to join up from villages, and by the end of September 1914 more than fifty towns had formed 'Pals' Battalions'. The 'Pals' were men and boys who lived and worked in the same neighbourhood. Many had gone to school together and included brothers and cousins.

There was a lot of excitement and chatter amongst the waiting men which John found encouraging. When Len and John got to the front of the queue the sergeant looked up from his desk. He was a tall, well-built man with a tanned complexion and a moustache that curled up at the sides. This made Len smile to himself, but he dared not show it. The sergeant's uniform was immaculate and his voice boomed out loudly at the two lads before him.

'Right, lads, let us see what we can do for you.'

Len explained that, if possible, he and John would like to stay together as long as they could.

'Well it will be impossible for me to promise anything on a long term basis but joining up together means we can send you to Aldershot Barracks to do your training together. I'm sure someone will look into you staying together for as long as possible. I want you to go through that door, over there on the left, where you will have a medical inspection. You will be weighed and a doctor will check that you are fit enough for active service. I doubt there will be any problems … let's hope not, anyway.

'After your medical you will be sent to be measured up for your uniforms. Once that's all done, all that's left is for you to sign on the dotted line. So I will see you back here when all that's finished with.'

The medical and fitting went well for both the lads. They signed the paperwork and that was that. They had joined the army; they were both given a 'Kings Shilling'. They stared at the tiny coin in their hands. Len felt very proud of himself and John was now feeling pretty pleased with himself too.

As the two lads descended the town hall steps back into the street, Len said, 'Let's celebrate with a pint, John. I think we deserve one, don't you?'

'Okay, mate,' said John.

John had been brought up in a Methodist family so alcohol was not really allowed, but he decided it was the start of him being an adult. So, provided he was sensible, he would dabble in these out of bounds activities. As it happened, he was not too keen on the taste of beer, but he didn't want to disappoint Len.

Len had a pint of beer while John had half a pint. The atmosphere in the pub was jovial. Lads were chatting about signing up and how they were hoping to make a difference out in France.

'They said it would be over by Christmas,' shouted one lad over the noise. 'My brother wrote to say that on Christmas day they put down their weapons and both sides met in no-man's land.'

'I heard they played football,' said another lad. 'It's a damn pity they didn't stay friends and put an end to this war.'

'Then none of us need have signed up today.'

'Well, all we can do, chaps, is get out there and show those Jerry bastards what for!'

A cheer went up from the new recruits. Many of the men ordered another drink to celebrate that last remark, but Len and John left the pub and headed for home.

John needed to get home to talk to his mother and try to reassure her that he had made the right decision. He knew it was not going to be an easy task.

'Here you are, Mam. The King's Shilling!' said John as he placed the new shiny coin on the table.

'So you've been and done it then? Signed yourself up to this dreadful war with no second thought of your ole mam, struggling on her own!' She placed her head in her hands and started to cry. John hated these sorts of confrontations. He was worried he would say the wrong thing.

'Mam, that's not fair. They are so short of men signing up that soon it will become compulsory. I had to sign up and help out as best I can.'

'And get yourself killed, no doubt.'

This felt like a dagger to John's heart. He went outside and slammed the door behind him. Why couldn't his mam be more supportive? He shuddered. Yes, he might be killed, but he hoped to get a job away from the front line. He knew that stretcher-bearers didn't carry weapons and he was concerned about having to kill people. He was not a conscientious objector, he was not refusing to go away to war, but the thought of killing someone really played on his mind. How would he ever forgive himself?

The door opened and John's mam came and put her arms around her son. 'I'm sorry, lad. We say things in haste that we don't mean to. You will make a fine soldier. I'll put your King's Shilling in a pot on my bedside table, and every night I shall take it out and pray to God to keep you safe.'

John was right - his mother had not taken it at all well. John, her only son, was going away to war. His father had been killed during the first year, 1914. She only had John to lean on and to care and provide for her. But she realised that deep down there was nothing she could do about the situation she found herself in. She knew that, as far as he could, Len would keep an eye on her boy.

Ernest and Beatrice decided it would be a good idea to have a get together for the two friends before they left. So with John's mum's help, they arranged a party in the local church hall. They enjoyed good food, good company, and played many party games. The whole evening was a huge success.

Everything went to plan and within two weeks the boys were on their way to Aldershot. They headed for the railway station; this would be a longer journey for Len than going into Leicester. Both men were feeling excited. They had never travelled very far from Leicester. Len and John were both looking smart in their new uniforms, complete with kit bags. They were excited at this new prospect and where it would lead them.

Chapter Two

Christmas 1915

And so Christmas 1915 came around. A lot of troops doing their training were coming home for Christmas. Some soldiers had been home during that year due to injuries and illnesses but for those coming home for the first time it was an exciting time.

Families all over Britain had spent several weeks preparing for this festive season. Mincemeat had been made and put into jars, puddings had steamed for hours on the hob, and cakes had been made in the scullery and stored in the larder in airtight tins ready to be iced. Homes were filled with the aroma of spices, cinnamon, cloves and nutmeg reminding families of happy childhood Christmases.

For many this special family holiday would never be the same again. Mothers and fathers had lost sons, wives had lost husbands, brothers and cousins all lost to the brutal war being fought miles away in France.

The lads from Aldershot were looking forward to going home to spend this exceptional time with their families, knowing that, come the New Year, they would be getting ready to go to France and face whatever life would throw at them. They felt apprehensive but knew they must concentrate on having the best Christmas ever.

The railway station at Aldershot was extremely busy with soldiers waiting for the trains to arrive. There was noise all around as excited men chattered amongst themselves about going home. Soon the train arrived and everyone rushed to get a seat. Len and John were lucky. As they squeezed into a carriage, they placed their kit bags on the already crowded luggage rack.

They chatted excitedly on the train journey home. Len had bought his mother a beautiful small robin ornament that he knew she would love. John had put together some chocolates and rather nice biscuits for his mother and him to share. Len had bought his sister, May, a pretty bracelet — he knew how she loved jewellery. For Stanley he had bought a notebook, and he had bought pipe tobacco for his father.

John's mother was so pleased to see her boy looking so well.

'Well, lad, this army life really suits you. I've never seen you looking so perky! It's great to have you home. Now let's get you a cup of tea and dinner will be ready about five.'

John sat himself down by the kitchen fire and was surprised to find he was nodding off to sleep, despite his mother's constant chatter.

Len's mother was delighted to see her son home. She hugged him then held him at arm's length as she looked at him.

'It's so lovely to have you home — and my, how well you look. It has been nice receiving your letters. Life sounds very busy for you.'

'Yes, busy, but I'm surprised how I have taken to army life, Mother. The training is tough — we dig trenches, practise with guns and bayonets, do lots of PT. I do enjoy the route marches: we march for miles. They certainly put us through our paces.'

'Your father should be home soon. He is so looking forward to seeing you, Leonard. I think he has missed you working alongside him in the shop.'

'I'll go upstairs and unpack this kit bag; it takes up so much room.'

Len went up to his familiar bedroom. He unpacked and sat on the bed, contemplating how much his life had changed since he was last here reading about that tragic railway accident all those weeks ago. He heard the back door open and close and heard his father's deep voice. He waited to give his mother time to have a word with her husband then slowly made his way down the stairs. His father looked at him then shook him by the hand.

'My word, look at you! My boy has grown into a man. I couldn't be any more proud of you, son.'

'You two go into the lounge, there's a fire been lit in there. I'll finish getting the dinner and I will bring you both a cup of tea in a minute or two.'

Beatrice watched with pride as her eldest son and her husband turned their backs on her and walked through the door.

May and Stanley, Leonard's sister and younger brother, arrived home from school. May was an attractive girl, slim and tall with dark shiny hair and similar looks to her mother. Stanley, on the other hand, was small for his age. He had almost black wavy hair and a sullen look about him. He was a serious child and didn't mix very well, even in the confines of his own family. May was delighted to see her elder brother. She hugged him and was eager to know how he had been getting on.

After their evening meal, the family returned to the lounge. Len was the centre of attention, but the warmth and comfort of home suddenly made him feel very tired and, like John, he soon started to feel very sleepy.

'Well, if you don't mind, I'm ready to call it a day and get my head down.'

'Yes, I'm feeling tired too,' said May, 'so I think I will retire. Good night.' She went over and kissed both her parents on the cheek. She didn't bother to kiss her disgruntled brother, Stanley.

'Yes, Stanley, it will soon be past your bed time,' said his mother gently.

And so the evening in the Folwell household came to an end. Ernest went and stood outside to smoke his pipe. It felt so good to have his family all together under one roof again, but what did the future hold? He would make sure his family had a special Christmas together this year.

Christmas Eve came around and a lot of the families from Woodhouse Eaves met in the church, as they had done for hundreds of years, to join in the annual neighbourhood carol singing. The Vicar had a good strong voice and had run a church choir for the past few years, so the singers were in good voice. Wrapped in warm winter clothing to keep out the cold evening air, they made their way around the village singing the familiar Christmas carols.

John and Len's families all joined in this special event. John's favourite carol was, 'While Shepherds Watched Their Flocks by Night.' He sang with gusto and his proud mother joined him.

May enjoyed singing 'Away in a Manger.' She had enjoyed playing Mary in the school nativity play. Stanley had been a shepherd. Stanley really enjoyed the evening. He loved to be outdoors, especially in the evening. When it was dark it made him feel mysterious. The elderly people came to their doors and windows to watch the singers. They smiled and waved, reminded of Christmases past.

The Manor House had only three servants these days; the housekeeper, cook and general maid, whose job it was to clear fires, make beds, and care for the upkeep of the house. Lord and Lady Greyson encouraged their staff to go out and join in the carol singing with the villagers. Molly, the maid, took quite a shine to John, who blushed every time he noticed her looking at him. Len nudged John and whispered 'Looks like you have an admirer, mate.'

Every year it was the tradition to finish up at the Manor House. Lord and Lady Greyson had enjoyed entertaining the villagers since they had moved there. As soon as Stanley entered the large hall his face lit up and his head tipped back to look up at the amazing sight in front of him. The huge Christmas tree almost reached the ceiling, decorated with red and gold ornaments and small white candles. Stanley looked at it in wonder. He never tired of seeing this magical sight.

A long table was set out with a delicious spread of food. Candles and vases of holly with red berries were set at intervals along the table. Sherry was served in cut crystal glasses and mead was served to the men.

The whole evening was a huge success and, as the tired villagers made their way home, it started to snow.

'Look, everyone,' shouted Len. 'It looks like we're going to have a white Christmas. Happy Christmas everyone. See you at church in the morning.'

A cheer went up as a band of happy people made their way home.

On Christmas morning the snow outside had settled. The sun was shining making the frost glisten like tiny stars in distant galaxies. The church was full and the singing was loud and clear. Lord and Lady Greyson stood in the church porch and gave all the children a carefully wrapped Christmas present as they left the church.

Lord Greyson was a retired doctor. He was rather a stout man with a kind red face. His smile could light up a room. He enjoyed running the Quorn Hunt of which he was Master. He organised the meetings with the hounds. Many horses had been sent out to France for the War effort, but locally there were enough horses to form part of the hunt. It was a spectacular sight watching gentlemen in hunting pink following the hounds, chasing across the open countryside

Lady Greyson had worked as a nurse in Guy's Hospital in London, where she had met her husband. She was tall and elegant, had fair hair and rather attractive brown eyes.

Before they moved to live in Woodhouse Eaves, Agnes Greyson had been part of the Women's Suffragette Movement. She hadn't tied herself to the railings in Downing Street or been thrown into jail, but she had attended some of Emmeline Pankhurst's meetings and hoped that eventually women would get the vote. With the outbreak of the Great War, the movement had taken a back seat and lots of well to do ladies had signed up to become nurses and volunteer with the Voluntary Aid Department to help with the war effort. In the village of Woodhouse Eaves, Agnes had set up a ladies' group at the Manor House to knit socks and jumpers and arrange for parcels to be sent to the front, knowing that lots of men would be only too pleased to receive them.

☐ *VAD stands for Voluntary Aid Detachment. They were often women from middle class families who volunteered their services to help out in base hospitals in both Britain and France, working alongside military nurses. They were organised by the Red Cross and in later years the Order of St. John.*

Chapter Three

<u>The Journey</u>

Back at the barracks it was all stations go.

'Right,' shouted Sergeant Anderson. 'Are we ready for action, men?'

A shout of, 'Yes, sar'nt' ' echoed around the room.

'Come on then, let's get on with the job in hand.'

Anderson was strict but fair with these young men and they trusted him with their lives. They set off from the comfort of the barracks in Aldershot that had been home for the last six months, and boarded the army issue bus — green-grey in colour, good for camouflage they were told.

It was a dull, cold January day as the men arrived at the south coast port of Southampton. The quayside was packed with soldiers in uniform. Some were hugging loved ones as they said a final goodbye, while others were smoking and chatting amongst themselves. At last it was time to board the Manchester Importer Steamer and head off for Le Havre on the French Coast.

'My, it's a bit of a crush, John,' shouted Len above the noise and bustle.

Before too long the ship was full and ready for the off. With a blast of her horn, in the late afternoon mist, the ship set sail out into the English Channel. In the fading light a cross wind got up and started a swell. The ship started to roll.

Some of the men managed to sleep. Others went up on deck to get some fresh air and many were seasick over the sides. The men had a fitful night. Len and John talked quietly to each other until tiredness overtook them both.

After disembarkation, the tired men stretched their weary bodies.

'Right!' shouted the sergeant. 'Let's go over to the canteen to get something to eat. I know some of you won't feel like eating yet but it's going to be a few hours before your next meal.'

The men crowded into the warm canteen and those feeing well enough to eat enjoyed bacon and eggs with fried bread and toast and a strong cup of tea. Some of the men thought it better to make do with a slice of toast and a glass of water.

Le Havre was a busy port filled with both cargo and naval vessels and the quayside was once again filled with army personnel. There were a few hours to wait for the tide to come in to fill the Seine basin. The men boarded a hospital ship on its way back to Rouen having dropped its injured and ill men back   in Southampton. From there the soldiers would be sent to the Netley Hospital to recover. And so the voyage up the River Seine to Rouen began.

For the soldiers who stayed awake, the scenery reminded them of river scenes at home. Of childhood days playing in the fields, making dens, climbing trees, collecting the pale blue eggs of blackbirds, pricking a hole in both ends of the egg and blowing out the yolk to preserve the shell. One or two of the lads wished they were children again, free as the birds in spring, reliving their youth. But there was a job to be done, a war to be won. They must do their best for King and Country. They wanted everyone at home to be proud of them.

Occasional wisps of smoke could be seen in the distance. Often a church spire stood tall out of the mist indicating a small village or hamlet. Tall chateaux with windows boarded up for the winter stood in their own barren gardens. They passed woods and fields dotted with sheep or cattle.

One of the men started singing, 'It's a long way to Tipperary; it's a long way to go.'

The rest of the men joined in and the cheerful singing combined with the beautiful scenery and the pale winter sunlight soon lifted the tired men's spirits.

After leaving the quayside in Rouen the men marched through the town. They had been instructed by the sergeant to march in silence until they were out of the town. They marched down narrow streets with old wooden houses. The timber had warped over the years and one or two of the houses seemed to lean on the others. They passed the cathedral with its marvellous ornate statues of saints, its exquisite pieces of pure flamboyant stone work, its pinnacles pointing upwards and majestic stained glass windows and soaring towers.

They passed the cross where Joan of Arc was burnt at the stake. Len shivered as he thought about the terrible death for a young lady. A group of men sat outside a bar and as the soldiers passed, the proprietor, wearing his apron, shouted in French, 'C'est bon de te voir les gars' (It's good to see you, lads).

As they got to the outskirts of the town of Rouen the living conditions were not good. The streets were dirty and young urchins ran around in rags. An old woman held out her hands, begging.

A flurry of snow descended on the men as they left the city behind. A young lad called Pete let out a sneeze as the snowflakes tickled his nose.

'Bless you,' shouted Len. The men started to chatter to each other.

In the distance they could see the camp and Pete shouted, 'Look, lads, we're nearly there.' A cheer echoed across the French countryside.

Once in camp, the men were shown their tents and sleeping quarters. They were pleased to put down their heavy kit bags. They then enjoyed a meal of bully beef, cabbage, mashed potatoes and gravy.

'Right,' shouted the sergeant, 'you have done really well to have travelled this far. Get a good night's sleep. Lights out in this camp is 21.30, so I suggest you get to bed as soon as you can. I will see you after reveille at 06.30 tomorrow morning.'

A groan was heard from the men. Despite this, they were more than pleased to get to bed and get decent night's sleep.

The day arrived when the men had to decide what they were going to do next. They had various forms to fill out. Len scratched his head with his pencil. Clerk typist was what he was used to doing at home for the church, so he selected that option on his form.

'Well,' asked Len, 'what was your choice John?'

'Ambulance driver. You know how much I enjoyed driving Uncle Percy's car at home.'

'That was a smart choice,' replied Len. 'I know how you liked driving fast. You scared the wits out of me on that back road from Woodhouse Eaves to Leicester.'

Several of the men, Len included, were designated to work on the ambulance trains. First they had to spend two to three weeks at the Rouen field hospitals. These were set up in tents on the large horse racing compound as the main base hospitals in the town were getting too full. Despite the tents being large and basic, they were run efficiently.

It was the task of the new recruits to learn as much as they could about first aid, in order to help nurse the injured men.

Chapter Four

<u>The Training</u>

After breakfast a group of soldiers met in the hospital ready to start their training.

The Medical officer (MO) and two nursing sisters took the recruits into a side room. 'Good morning, everyone' said the MO as he acknowledged the new recruits.

'Good morning.' replied the men in unison

'Right, men. Sadly you will witness some horrific injuries, lots of terrible sights and illnesses on this job, but try not to dwell on this. Your work will be to comfort the men you come into contact with. We will show you how to dress their wounds and keep them comfortable — you can only do your best. I want you to remove yourselves from the situation when you go off duty. It's the only way you will survive in one piece. Some of our men who come in with injuries and illness are found to have venereal diseases.' He noticed some of the new younger recruits looking puzzled.

'They have sexually transmitted diseases,' added the nurse.

'Yes, this may take you by surprise but our troops have needs and there are 'ladies of the night' in our French towns and villages who are out to make a bit of money. Some of the troops have gonorrhoea and some have syphilis; neither very nice illnesses at all. The punishment for these men is they don't get paid whilst under our care. This is punishment enough - I don't want any of these men treated any differently to the rest. Are there any questions? '

Len put his hand up — it reminded him of school. 'Will we have help to change the dressings? 'he asked.

'Yes, you will, but over time you will develop enough confidence to do the dressings on your own. If you are ever in any doubt, always ask one of the nurses to show you what to do. You will have more nurses than doctors working on the ambulance trains with you.'

Len and John were sent to the busy hospital tent. 'This is Kate; she is one of our nurses. What I want you to do is take down the names of the men coming in for care. You will also prioritise who needs the most urgent care first.'

Kate was dressed in a white nurse's uniform with a starched white cap; she was a petite lady with doll like features - large, hazel eyes beneath long lashes and auburn hair put up in a bun.

She shook hands with both of the men and led them towards the doors where the men were waiting to be admitted. As Len and John looked at them, they were surprised to see how many men were waiting and how they were all being patient despite the urgency for medical attention.

Len held the blank page and started to note down the men's names. Kate told him what the injuries were, so he noted that down as well. John gently moved each patient to the ward where the men were sorted into categories. Some came in on stretchers, others limping and holding on to the nearest man available. Some of the soldiers were crying out in pain, some became aggressive, some men had vacant shocked looks about them; it was all rather harrowing for these new recruits.

John felt quite unwell as the injured men filed past him. He had never seen anything like it before. Kate reassured the injured men as they filed past. She became aware that John was not coping too well.

'Go and get yourself a cup of tea and come back in half an hour.' she said. I know it's difficult seeing all of these nasty injuries, but I'm afraid it's part of war. The not so nice side I'm afraid'.

After work Len and John went to the canteen for a bite to eat. 'Len, I'm not sure I'm ever going to get used to this. How are you feeling?'

'It's not easy lad but it's a job that needs doing, John.'

Len ate his dinner but John picked at his food.

'Come on John, I'm sure we will get used to it given time. Let's go down to the Y.M.C.A. hut and see what's going on down there. We need something to take our minds off things tonight,'

The next day Len and John worked on the hospital wards. Bandages needed changing, wounds needed cleaning, and men needed feeding and comforting. Len sat next to Charlie, who had suffered from gas inhalation. He coughed and spluttered as he desperately tried to clear his lungs. He was better propped up on pillows than lying flat. Charlie knew he was dying.

'Tell my mother and father I love them very much. Tell them I didn't suffer — I don't want Mother to worry.'

Len felt a lump in his throat as he held the young man's hand. 'I will tell them,' he said. 'You rest now. I will say a prayer for you.

'Please, dear Lord, take care of Charlie. Take away his pain and suffering as only you can. Be with his parents and siblings. Bring them all comfort at this sad time. Amen.'

Charlie whispered, 'Amen.' He sighed one last painful breath and died.

That night Len wrote home to Charlie's parents, telling them what a brave young man their son was and to be proud of him. 'His suffering is now over and, like you all, I won't forget him.'

Many of the injured soldiers had not changed their uniforms for several weeks and the smell, mixed with blood and gore, made Len retch.

'Come on' said a friendly nurse, 'I'll show you what to do and how to cope with it all.'

With a large pair of scissors she started to cut the wool uniform from the soldier, Robert's body, being careful of his wounds. Once the uniform was removed, she told Len to fetch a large bowl of warm, soapy water so that he could be washed.

'First take the uniform to the incinerator. Burning it is the only way to get rid of the stench and the fleas.'

Robert apologised.

'No,' said the nurse kindly, 'this isn't your fault. You will feel so much better when Len has washed you. We will both then attend to your wounds.'

Within an hour, Robert was clean, his wounds had been attended to and he was given his first proper meal for a week or more.

That evening Len went and asked Robert how he was feeling.

'Well, my leg wound is sore but I feel so much better after my wash and brush up. Thank you so much for your help.
'

'That's okay,' said Len. 'I'm new to all this. They are getting us ready to work on the ambulance trains, so it's all good practice. Get a good night's sleep and I will see you in the morning.'

Again Len and John met after work.

'How are you getting on John?'

'I've had a much better day today Len, I washed and bed bathed one or two soldiers, then I helped serve up the meals and fed some of the men who needed help. Despite their dreadful injuries, they are so grateful. I'm hungry. I don't know about you Len?'

'Yes let's go and see what's on the menu tonight.'

Len was hoping to find Robert a lot better when he went on duty the following morning; but Robert was delirious with a high temperature and a thumping headache.

'Hello, 'said Kate, the nurse who had encouraged Len the day before. 'I'm afraid Robert has gone down with trench fever. We need to keep him comfortable until I can arrange for him to be transported to the Base Hospital at Le Havre. From there, Robert will go by hospital ship to England and then on by ambulance train to the nearest hospital to his home.'

'I'm really sorry,' said Len. 'He was so grateful yesterday and to see him so Ill this morning is quite a shock.'

'I know. The best you can do for Robert is to cool his head and keep him comfortable. When the MO does his rounds he will prescribe some quinine which should help with his temperature and pain.'

Within a few days Len was saying goodbye to Robert, who was still quite fragile.

'I can never thank you enough,' said the brave solider.

'You get home and get better, that's all I ask,' replied Len and with that Robert was carried away on a stretcher for his long journey home.

The more the latest recruits did, the easier it became. But sometimes keeping your cool was difficult.

A scream was heard from the hospital corridor and the scene that met the orderlies was shocking. A soldier with part of his face missing and his brain protruding from his head was a horrendous sight for even the most hardy medical staff. The patient was gently guided by the stretcher bearers into the operating theatre. Two surgeons worked for over an hour, but the young man tragically lost his life.

By the end of the first week the lads were pleased to get a day off. They set off after breakfast to have a look around the city of Rouen. They found the café they had passed on the march through the city several weeks ago. They went inside and ordered a French coffee each. John found it was an acquired taste but Len enjoyed the whole French experience. They paid the 2 francs; it felt strange trying to work out the exchange rate from English money to French francs.

'Let's go and have a look around the Cathedral, we could maybe light a candle or two for the soldiers we have lost this last week or two.' said Len.

The two men entered the magnificent building. 'Wow its huge,' whispered an amazed John 'Look over there it looks like a service is being held.'

'Yes I believe you are right, let's sit here at the back for now.'

The two friends sat with their heads bowed. After ten minutes or so they decided to make their way to the front altar to light one or two candles. Len offered up a prayer for Charlie and thought of Robert on his way home. Both Len and John found this small act very moving.

Chapter Five

<u>A Day in the Life</u>

Not only did the new recruits work on the hospital wards but they occasionally tended the gardens too. This was a good time to enjoy the outdoors and have a well-earned break from the confines of the wards, Len was sent to clear up a piece of ground. He cleared away paper, orange peel and other rubbish that had been carelessly dropped. He then started to dig a pit with Private Bernard.

Bernard was a large fellow with light brown hair. He had a small beard and moustache and rather bad teeth. He had brown eyes that could sometimes look straight through you. He was quite serious but was enjoying his work in France.

'Come on, old chap; put your back into it,' remarked Len.

'I'm doing me best, and I'm not old, you know, only twenty.'

Len laughed. 'Once we have this job done we can knock off for dinner. I'm starving.'

'Oh dear. Don't look now but old Lanky is on his way over here.'

Private Hill was very tall, hence the nick name "Lanky". He walked with a slight stoop.

'How are you getting on chaps?' shouted Lanky from a distance.

'OK. We've nearly got this pit dug out and then we are going for dinner.'

'It's way too early for dinner, boys.'

'Well we've been at this job since eight thirty this morning so I think we're ready for a break. 'The men couldn't agree, so with a shrug of his shoulders Lanky left the men to it.

As soon as he had gone round the corner Len said, 'Come on, Bernard, let's go for lunch. He won't be coming back here until later.' So the two men downed tools and went to freshen up before dinner at 12.30. Dinner was bully beef and piccalilli.

'I can't stand Piccalilli,' said Bernard as he screwed up his nose.

'That's okay,' said Len as he scooped the portion of Piccalilli off of Bernard's plate onto his own.

Later on the two men went to the local general hospital, where they were instructed to scrub out a hospital tent that needed to be sent to the front line. This was quite a hard job and both men were up to their elbows in soap suds when a sergeant rushed into the tent and asked, 'Aren't you two R.A.M.C. (Royal Army Medical Core.) men? '

'Yes,' they replied.

'Well come along to Bay Office. An officer has fallen from his horse down on the beach. You need to find a stretcher, quick.'

There was no ambulance to be found in the camp, so the two men took a wheeled stretcher down to the beach. The trouble with the wheeled stretcher was that the wheels dug into the sand, so once the officer was on the stretcher the two men carried him. The stretcher was now quite heavy and the two men had a job to carry the load over the soft sand. Once on the path they were able to put the wheels down and wheel him up to the hospital, where a nurse took over from them.

It was decided that John would be best suited to work in the field hospital. He had become quite an asset to the busy ward and was happy to stay put where he felt at ease with what he was doing.

Diary entry; Sunday April 16th 1916

Sunday was sometimes a day of leisure, but more often than not there were jobs to be done. After the 07.00 am parade the men had half an hour before breakfast. Len, like a lot of other men, would go and have a lie down.

After breakfast which consisted of bacon, bread, jam and tea. Len cleaned up one of the coaches. He was then sent to K coach to clean the brasses and panels. This particular Sunday he went for a medical inspection which lasted three quarters of an hour.

Within another week it was time for Len, Bernard and another lad, Stanley, to join the ambulance trains. Stanley had also worked in the field hospitals and these three men and John had enjoyed their spare evenings down in the Y.M.C.A. hut. Stanley was mid height with brown deep set eyes and freckles across his nose. He had an infectious smile and was extremely amusing to be around. He was slightly bald and most of the time he wore a cap. He had a pale complexion with lines around both his mouth and eyes due to his constant smiling.

The three friends made their way to the busy railway station in Rouen to join up with their ambulance train. They boarded the train to have a look around. The wards were big enough to hold 30 patients in bunk beds three storeys high. The bottom bunk could be used for the less injured soldiers to sit on if not needed as a bed. The men found their sleeping carriage which was rather cramped but cosy, sleeping four people on two sets of bunk beds.

'Well it's a good job we are friends!' stated Len 'I bags one of the top bunk beds if that's alright with you chaps.'

'Yes I've no problem with that,' laughed Stanley as he lay on a bottom bunk.' It's quite cosy down here. Roll on bed time, I say.' The kitchen was in a separate carriage and was quite small but adequate.

So for these three men and the other new recruits spread around the long train, their work on ambulance train number six began.

The train had recently dropped off its injured troops. The dirty sheets had been taken off the bunk beds and the dark brown blankets folded and left at the bottom of each bed.

'Right, 'said an orderly dressed all in white. 'The beds have been left for you to make up. Here come the clean sheets now.'

Another man in a white uniform boarded the train with an armful of sheets. He placed them down on a bed near the door, smiled at the new recruits and left.

'I will show you how to make up this set of three beds,' the first orderly said as he pointed to the nearest set of bunk beds.' Then I will see how the three of you get on. It's a difficult job to start with, but after you have made up your first hundred it will be a piece of cake.' The three friends smiled at that last remark.

The men watched with interest. Soon the beds were pristine and ready for action.

'Right I will make another one or two up to help you, but now it's your turn. The three men made a start and within an hour the carriage was ready for use.

Chapter Six

Working on the Trains

Within a few days the three men were beginning to settle into their new job.

At 04.00 am on Friday 14th June 1916, ambulance train number six was at Vecquemont Station. The train was ready to pick up injured soldiers.

Most were stretcher cases that needed to be gently placed on the beds and made comfortable. First they picked up about 200 men from a field hospital, and then the train went on to the Casualty Clearing Station, which was set up near the front line. Most of these men had been operated on recently, so the ambulance train staff had to be made aware that these men needed extra care and attention.

One of Len's jobs was to get the patients some breakfast and a cup of tea. Years later, it amazed Len's family how thinly he could slice a loaf of bread. It was not until his diary came to light several years after Len had died that they fully understood.

Some of the men needed feeding which could be a difficult job as the train moved along the tracks. Often it caused the men to smile. 'It's bad enough being in this bloody bunk, never mind not getting fed properly!'

The nurses and orderlies enjoyed the times they could laugh with the men, but it was hard to see the seriously injured ones. Shrapnel wounds were terrible; not only was there a deep wound but the wound was burnt as the hot metal went into the delicate flesh. The pain from these wounds needed morphine, which only a doctor could administer to the patient.

Once the train was full it travelled to the base hospitals, where the injured men were stretchered off the train and onto the busy wards.

It was here that Len was able to catch up with John. If time allowed they would go for a walk or go to the canteen for a well-earned meal. John loved this time catching up with Len on how well they were both getting on.

'I heard from mother last week.' said an excited John. 'She has joined your mum and goes up to the Manor House twice a week to knit and wrap up parcels to send out to us. She seems very settled without me, I'm pleased to say.'

'Well that's brilliant.' replied Len. 'Yes it would be nice to receive some of those parcels from home sometime. Stanley received a parcel last week with home knitted socks in. They looked jolly warm. I wrote to Bert, Dick and Cath this week. It must be nice for them to hear from us. It's certainly does us good to receive their letters.'

It was Len, Bernard and Stanley's job, once their carriage was empty, to fold the blankets, change the dirty blood stained sheets, and wash the carriage out, disinfecting the floors and blood-splashed walls. Then the beds had to be made up with clean sheets ready for the next journey. They were always grateful when this job was done and they could go for a rest and meal.

Len puts in his diary, 'Got down to it,' which means he got ready to go to bed. He also spent this time writing letters and cards home to his friends and family. Len was delighted to receive parcels from home. His mother tried to send letters and parcels on a regular basis. The Red Cross also sent basic parcels out for the troops containing items for personal hygiene, such as toothpaste and brush, bars of Sunlight soap, tobacco and non-perishable food and sweets.

All the men enjoyed their time off work. They joined in football matches with the casual clearing stations or field hospital staff. Len enjoyed scoring for them and wrote about them in his Diary. The Y.M.C.A. put on very entertaining concerts. Len, John, Stanley and Bernard always made the most of these relaxing times together.

They also liked to walk round the local villages. They wished they could speak French so they could make conversation with the locals. But they decided a smile was the same in any language. The locals enjoyed seeing the British troops and there was often a cafe or two that offered freshly made French bread and pastries. The two friends were also alarmed to find that some of the larger villages had two brothels, a blue light brothel that was for the men from the higher ranks and a red light brothel for the Tommies and ordinary soldiers.

As the war progressed the villages began to suffer from the constant bombing and warfare. Families were forced to leave their homes, which became derelict, and often places where soldiers could hide away from the trenches.

Bernard was a bit of a loner especially after a day's work. He liked to go out for a walk. He had a good torch but of course he had to be careful. Any sight of a light shining out could be seen by the enemy and a sniper's bullet could be the end of you. He found this time relaxing. He could smoke his cigarette under the cover of his coat and think of his girlfriend, Freda, at home in Durham. He felt close to her in this quiet time. He would look at the moon, as he had told her to do, and somehow the moon developed a sort of soft face that smiled down at him. He was hoping to ask her to marry him on his next few days of leave. The trouble was he had no idea when his next leave would be or even if he would survive this damn war.

The following week all the lads were back to work and as busy as ever. Len had cleaned his carriage with the help of Bernard. The smell was fresh. Stanley had polished the brasses.

What a night they had: no peace, no break, the work was constant. They had been picking men up in Boulogne, and almost emptying the field hospital there.

There were men with broken legs, several amputees, one or two with arms blown to pieces; several with gangrene whose limbs most certainly would have to come off; lots of delicate tummy wounds, made from burning shrapnel; several had trench foot, a condition where the feet had not been dried and oiled for many days and the flesh had become so weak it started to peel off the men's feet. This could be a very serious condition — the feet had to be kept dry and clean and the dressings not put on too tight.

However were they going to manage? It was great that they had two nurses helping on the long trip back to Abbeville Base Hospital. But manage they did.

As usual, Len went and prepared a light meal for the more seriously wounded. He made scrambled egg that would be soft to eat and a good way of getting some goodness into these sick young men. The sandwiches were Len's speciality: thin slices of bread, buttered sparingly. Some were egg, others jam or honey and some were a finely grated French cheese. He boiled broth on the small stove — this would go well with the army-issue bread. Many of the men had not eaten properly for several days and with a hot cup of tea they could relax as best they could given the circumstances they found themselves in.

'Help me!' came a scream across the carriage.

Len rushed across to the man who had shouted.

'I can't breathe,' said the injured soldier. Stanley was now at Len's side.

'Let's sit you up a bit,' said Len kindly. The last thing he wanted was the young soldier having any sort of panic attack. If this happened the whole carriage could get upset.

'Let's get this young man into a sitting position, it will help him breath better. That's the trouble with the middle bunk, it can be quite claustrophobic.'

So the two men gently moved him into a sitting position. In a few minutes his panic had eased.

'Thank you chaps,' he said with a weak smile.

'Try to get some sleep, mate,' said Stanley as he pulled the blanket round the injured man. With that the reassured young man shut his eyes.

'Nothing hurts when you're asleep, does it?' he said.

'No, if you sleep as best you can now, it won't seem too long before we reach base.' Within ten minutes he was in a fitful sleep with a worried frown on his brow.

Another patient cried out in pain. Len went over.

'My legs are painful,' said Billy, 'can you give me something to ease the pain?'

'Let's have a look for you.' But as Len lifted the blanket off the young man's legs he was amazed to see that there were no legs there at all. Both of this young man's legs had been amputated from the knees down. 'I will see what I can organise for you,' said a worried Len as he placed the blanket down.

He found Sister Kate further down the ward. 'Can I have a word sister, please?'

'Yes, I'll be with you in a minute.'

The minute seemed to stretch out a long time as Len waited.

'Right,; said Kate, 'what can I do for you?'

Len explained the situation to Kate. She responded. 'Yes, it's quite usual in these cases, the patient can still feel his legs that have been amputated. Let me come over and explain it to him. The shock of what has actually happened has not really sunk in yet, poor lad.'

With that he followed Kate back up the ward. 'Right, young man. Let us have a look at you.

'It's this pain in my legs, sister, it won't go away.'

Kate put her hand on the young man's shoulder as she gently reminded him of his injuries. 'But why can I still feel pain?' he asked in bewilderment. 'That can't be right.'

'Well, Billy, your body has not come to terms with this yet; your injuries are new, you are not used to the idea that you have no legs beyond the knee. The surgery is still so recent and the nerves still believe they are there. I know it's hard for you at this moment in time, but your wounds will heal. You will be fitted with artificial limbs so you can walk again. For now your war is over. But this has been a life-changing event for you. You are alive and will be going home as soon as possible.'

The young man gave out an angry shout. 'It's not bloody fair. Why me? I'm sorry, nurse, but I will never get used to this.'

'It's hard to accept, I know, but you are alive. That's the main thing. We will give you something for the pain; Len will bring it to you in a minute.

'But why give him something for the pain that's not really there?' asked Len as they walked away from the bed.

'It will help with his pain; it is more psychological as well,' said Kate. 'If he thinks he has been given something, mentally it will help him.'

Len gave him two tablets, 'Here you are, lad. You take these with this cup of water. I will be bringing you something to eat shortly.'

'Thank you.'

'Try and get yourself comfortable.' The soldier shifted his heavy body with tears rolling down his cheeks.

Len went over to Ken. 'I've come to change the dressings on your feet. Let's have a look how they are doing.' It made Len's stomach turn as the dirty dressing fell off Ken's feet. He put the dirty dressing into a bag then went to wash his hands before he prepared the clean dressings.

'Well they seem to be healing fairly well,' said Len. 'How did they get into this state?'

'Well,' said Ken, 'we'd been in the trench for well over a week. The conditions were cold and the mud got worse as the rain fell incessantly. It started to cover our boots, and once your boots are soaking wet it's hard to take them off to dry your feet, only to put back on your wet boots — so I'm afraid I didn't bother. I wish I had now as this isn't nice. But you know the conditions in the trenches are pretty dreadful. We are wet, we can't sleep, we can't get warm; we huddle up close at nights and then, of course, the fleas have a field day almost eating us alive. And the rats! You have never seen rats as big as the ones in our trench. Poor old Corporal got bitten on the tips of his fingers by the rats, made him really ill it did. And the stench from the corpses we can't bury. It's too dangerous, so they just pile up in a heap.'

'That sounds dreadful,' said Len, so thankful that he was working in warm comfortable conditions and not out in the front line trenches.

Bernard walked over to Len. 'Come here a minute.'
'What's up, mate?'

'You know the Officer the one over there near the door.'

'Yes.'

'Well don't look now, but I reckon he's popped his clogs, so to speak. But I don't want to alarm the other patients.'

'I'll go over and have a look. If he has died I will cover him up as best I can so the others think he's sleeping. However we must alert the doctor as soon as possible to put down what he died of on his death certificate.'

When Len came back to see Bernard he said, 'Yes you were right. We must contact the doctor at the next railway station and get the body off the train as soon as we can. It's a sad affair but unfortunately that's war.'

At the next station Len and Bernard got off the train to stretch their legs, while Kate the Nurse went to J carriage to fetch a doctor.

'The best thing is to take the body back to Abbeville - there is a mortuary there. Take him off first and the other patients won't notice. Leave his two dog tags on so that the people at the mortuary can identify who he is. The round one will be left on the body, but the eight sided one will be taken off so his name, rank number and religion can be recorded. I will contact the hospital and tell them that we are on the way.'

Chapter Seven

<u>Zeppelins</u>

The train slowed to an almost stop and Len wondered why he. Looked out of the carriage window and the scene before him made him gasp with horror.

'Oh my word,' he stammered louder than he had intended.

'What's up mate? 'asked Stanley as he made his way across the carriage.

Len found it hard to put into words. For the first time in his life he saw a Zeppelin hovering over the French countryside. This unusual machine was hideous and so large. Len had never seen anything like it. He had seen postcards and newspaper reports but never seen one in real life.

It was a Zeppelin that had first bombed London from the air in May 1915, killing seven and injuring 35. Luckily for the people of London it bombed during the night so not many people would have seen this hideous machine.

Len beckoned to Stanley as he made his way to the door. His face was ashen.

'Come and have a look at this sight out here. I've never seen anything like it before!' Now several of the injured soldiers were looking out of the windows.

'Oh My Lord!' said Tony, lying on his back with two broken legs. 'We saw one or two of those while we were in the trenches but they were a lot higher than that one. I believe they can float about two miles high. How threatening that one looks.'

The weary men craned their necks to see what was going on. The train was about to enter a tunnel so the train driver pulled slowly into it for safety, a bomb dropped from that height would certainly cause a lot of damage. The great train let out a lot of steam as it ground to a halt.

Len and Stanley climbed down from the carriage and walked to the entrance of the tunnel. The large machine overhead made a soft whirling sound.

'Goodness me, I never knew how enormous they were.'

By now Len and Stanley had been joined by Sister Kate. She stood as close to the men as she could as she felt extremely frightened.

She tried to stop her voice from trembling. 'Look, you can see the silhouette of people in the caravan thing underneath.'

The great machine in the sky hardly made a noise as it floated away over the fields.

'Well' said Stanley, 'The German army and navy both have Zeppelins designed by Count Ferdinand Von

Zeppelin, hence the name. They were built as a look out and also useful to the navy as they float at a great height over the sea and spot submarines where ships can't. They also carry bombs and when travelling at night are hard to spot, because they are so high and make very little noise. The one good thing is that they are easily shot down. The hydrogen gas inside the inner membrane catches fire and the whole thing goes up in flames extremely quickly.'

'How extraordinary!' said an interested Len.

They watched the great machine as it sailed away into the distance.

'Let's get back to the job in hand, hey lads?' said Len as he turned away and walked back to the train. 'I'll go and get the tea on. I bet the lads are getting hungry.'

Len climbed into the kitchen wagon, but then realised as the train started to move that he would be stuck there, not able to get back to his ward. Not to worry, he thought, I will prepare the tea for the men and have my tea while I'm in here. That's all I can do until we stop at the next station.

The kitchen wagon was small and once tea had been made he leaned against the wall and watched out of the window. The smoke swirled past the window into the distance, as muddy fields and weary looking horses made their way to the front line. Black burnt out trees stood stark against the cloudy sky. Would this war torn country ever recover? Len thought to himself.

They passed a canal and Len saw a hospital barge painted grey with a white square and a large bright red cross. They had the same symbol on the side of the train. This was to signify these were not fighting vessels but transporting sick and injured men. The boatman driving the barge waved and Len waved back and smiled.

At the next stop Len got out from his kitchen and took the tea into his patients.

'I began to think we had left you stranded at the tunnel,' said a smiling Stanley.

'Well I've had my tea so you go and get yours while I feed the men. I bet you're all ready for a nice cup of tea, aren't you lads? '

'Yes, more than ready,' said Tony. 'We are really quite parched.'

'Tea coming up.'

Without a lot of bother Len served the tea up to the men. One patient had a gunshot wound to his face, so Stanley tried as best he could to feed the hungry man. It was hard for him to swallow and Stanley was rather worried the liquid would go into his lungs. It made more sense to give him softened food which would be easier to swallow.

'That's better, lad, let's get some goodness into you. It will make you stronger. There is a very good doctor who specialises in reconstructive surgery, Doctor Harold Gillies. He will soon have you looking as good as ever.' It would take many skin grafts and surgeries to repair the soldier's face. Stanley made him comfortable and placed a clean dressing over the nasty wound. The doctor gave him an injection of morphine, letting him get a few hours free from pain and able to sleep.

At the next station they took on more injured troops.

'This is my cousin, Harry,' said one of the field hospital nurses. 'He has serious burns on his hands resulting from rescuing an injured soldier from a burning trench. Take good care of him for me, won't you?'

'Yes,' said Len. 'I will go and get some iodine and see about getting some painkillers down him. A clean dressing will stop him getting an infection. Don't you worry, lass, we will take good care of him!'

The nurse kissed Harry on the cheek. 'You take good care, lad; you're in the best of hands here. I will write to Aunt Lucy and let her know how you are. '

'Thank you. You have cared for me very well. Who would have thought that my young cousin Mabel would make such a fine nurse? I hope to catch up with you again soon when this bloody war is over.'

Len fetched clean dressings and soon had Harry's hands bound.

'They are so sore,' said a distressed Harry

'I will get the doctor to give you a strong painkiller.'

'Put that soldier over there on the top bunk then fill the carriage from the back.' Len said to a couple of stretcher bearers

'This man is in a pretty bad state. It might be better if he goes on a lower bunk.'

'Yes, that's fine. I will get the doctor to have a look at him sooner rather than later.' The carriage was almost full of injured men, which kept the staff very busy.

The next stop, at a casualty clearing station, Bernard got out of the train to see what needed doing. The night before, the casualty clearing station had taken a direct hit. The patients had been moved to a nearby barn for safety. 'We could do with another pair of hands here I'm afraid.' said a busy doctor as he left the barn, having heard the ambulance train come to a standstill. 'Let me see what we can do,' said Bernard as he turned to head back to the train. After a short discussion between the Doctor, Len and Stanley (from M coach) it was decided that Bernard could stop and help out.

This was new territory for Bernard, but was very similar to the work in the field hospitals and on the train. The only difference was that these injured soldiers had only recently been transported from the nearby trenches by the busy stretcher bearers. They were still in extreme shock and pain, needing urgent medical attention and pain relief.

The night was very long, but Bernard did his best in the most difficult of circumstances. 'Go and get yourself a hot drink. We will have some more staff arriving when the ambulance calls to pick up the wounded.'

It was two hours later that the train arrived at Rouen. The stretcher bearers waited patiently on the platform. Once the train was unloaded it was time to strip the sheets off the beds and prepare the carriage for the next journey.

Len fetched buckets of hot water so they could wipe the bunk beds down and remove any traces of blood or mud. Stanley helped with this job unless he was wanted somewhere else. Once the beds were made up again, Len started washing the floors. The two men always felt relieved once the carriage was ready for action again. They were also hungry by this time and made their way to the canteen for their dinner.

After dinner the two men would often meet up with other colleagues. Len often met up with John when they were in the right area. John was still getting on so much better than he ever thought he would. He chatted to Len about his work in the field hospital. He was now able to tend many of the wounds on his own. Len was amazed how this shy young man had now grown in confidence.

This time together gave the three men a break from the horrors they had witnessed.

The whole of the British Army was in for a shock. On 5th June 1916 the news came through that Lord Kitchener had died. He was on his way to Russia to meet up with the Tsar for negotiations, when the ship he was in, the HMS Hampshire, hit a storm off the Orkneys. It then hit a German mine. The huge armoured vessel sank in fifteen minutes with no time to lower the lifeboats. Only fourteen crew reached the rocky shore, with six hundred and forty three lost, including Lord Kitchener.

Kitchener had encouraged so many men to sign up for the War that morale among the men was sober for a few weeks after the announcement.

Chapter Eight

<u>Stretcher Bearers</u>

Gunfire and explosions crashed around them. The cries of the wounded urged stretcher bearers, Martin and Colin, on. Courageously they negotiated no-man's land, dodging bullets and conquering their fears as they made their way through the squelching mud to the Tommie's who needed their help.

An horrific sight met them. Broken bodies lay everywhere, blood and gore spilled out of unconscious men, whilst others wept with the agony they were in.

Trying to reassure, Martin called out to a soldier whose knee was smashed by a bullet, 'We will be with you soon, mate. Hang on.' The rough terrain was hard work as the two men carrying the folded stretcher fell into a shell hole.

'Keep going, mate, it's not too far to go now. Lift her up a bit higher. That's it. We're nearly there.'

The folded stretcher was placed next to the injured soldier.

'Here we are, lad, let's help you up. That's good. Now hold on tight while we get you back to the trench.'

It was not easy with the weight they were carrying, but both men held onto the stretcher handles tightly. The last thing they wanted was to lose their patient in the mud. Over another ridge and they dropped down into the nearest trench.

'Let's see if we can stop that bleeding,' said Martin as he opened his kit bag, containing his first-aid kit. He fetched out a long, clean bandage and tied it tightly just above the knee. He pulled as tight as possible and noticed the gushing blood had almost stopped. The injured soldier had, by this time, passed out.

'Right, let's go along this trench as quickly as we can to the dressing station in that nearby barn.' It was difficult to get past the troops waiting to go over the top as the soldiers pressed their bodies into the mound of earth.

The mud and the slippery duck boards lining the base of the trenches made the short journey hard work.

'Hold on tight, lad, we are nearly there.' They put the stretcher down as Martin went into the makeshift barn.

'We have a soldier with a nasty knee injury, where are we to put him?' asked Martin.

'Put him just inside the door on the left and we will get one of our doctors to have a look at him.' said Bernard 'How are things out there?'

'Chaotic and very dangerous in no-man's land. We take a risk with our own lives, but there is a job to be done. We must get back, there are so many men needing our help. Bye for now, lad, you're in safe hands.'

With that, Martin picked up the now-empty stretcher and headed back the way he had come. Bernard made the injured soldier more comfortable as he assessed his wounds. 'Here comes one of our nurses. She will have a look at you and decide what to do next.'

Outside the two stretcher bearers were making their way back down the trenches. 'Here, lads, stop and have a hot drink,' said a friendly sergeant as he passed across two tin mugs full of hot steaming tea. Martin and Colin took the mugs and enjoyed the sweet hot liquid. The Padre made his way down the trench.

'It's only me boys,' he whispered. It was the Reverend Theodore Hardy. He was dedicated to his position on the front line and had spent many a night next to a wounded soldier comforting him until help arrived or death came.

'Here you are Padre, wrap yourself around this,' the sergeant said as he passed over a mug of hot tea. The Padre wrapped his hands around the mug.

'Thank you,' he said with a smile. 'It's been a long night out there. My feet feel so cold.' He stamped his feet and the mud splattered around him.

'Make sure you get those boots off sometime today, Padre, we don't want you going down with trench foot,' said a concerned Martin. 'Dry your feet well and find some dry socks; they have plenty of pairs at the advanced dressing station. Right, come on Colin, let's go and see who else we can save from this bloody mess. Thanks for the hot drink, Sarge.'

The two pals picked up the stretcher and headed back down the trench.

'Over here, mates, we have a soldier injured and caught up in the barbed wire. Here are some wire cutters; we will cover you as best we can from enemy fire.' Without another thought for their own safety both men climbed out of the trench.

As they got nearer the injured soldier Martin called out, 'Stop struggling! You are getting more tangled up. Try to stay still and we will soon have you off of the wire.' They noticed that the soldier had been shot in the arm and his face and hands were scratched from trying to escape.

Colin put the stretcher up on the other side of the wire, trying to put a barrier up to protect the three men. Luckily the wire cutters were sharp and after several cuts the wire fell away from the injured man.

'Right, are you okay to try and run back to the trenches? We will sort your arm out when we have you back.' the soldier nodded.

'You run back with this man and I'll carry the stretcher. I will give you a head start.' said Colin. Running as fast as they could the two men ran across the open terrain. One or two shots were heard as they continued to run. They dropped down into the muddy trench with a splash.

'Here, let's put a triangular bandage on that arm for support. I must then check how Colin is getting on.' Martin fetched a new triangular bandage out of his bag and carefully tied it around the young soldier's arm. He then told him to stay where he was while he looked over the top to see what Colin was doing.

Colin started to run across no-man's land half-carrying and half-dragging the stretcher. He dived into a shell hole as shots rang out from behind him. He lay winded for a few minutes while he got his breath back. It would be easier if he left the stretcher behind but they needed it to continue their work.

'Are you alright, mate?' a muffled voice asked.

'Yes, I think so. I will try again in a minute or two. You stay safe where you are.'

Colin tried again. He ran as low to the ground as he could. Another couple of shots were fired. This time Colin lay flat on the floor covered in mud. He edged his way across the ground. Within another few minutes he was back in the trench.

'Wow, that was a near miss,' he stated. 'How's our patient?'

'He's sitting further down the trench. I thought he would be safer down there. This soldier has offered to take him to the advanced dressing station. So we can get on here.

Back down the trench and another two Tommie's were found injured lying in the mud.

'Hold on, lads, we will be with you in no time.'

Again Martin and Colin went over the top. This time one of the soldiers had a shrapnel wound in his stomach. He was doubled over in pain, blood spurting out.

Colin looked in his bag and took out the largest dressing he could find. He lay the young man on his back and packed the sterile dressing into the open wound.

'He's in a bad way, this one,' said Colin. 'Let's take him back first and then come back for the other lad.'

Martin crept along to the other soldier. 'We will be back with you as soon as we can. Your leg injury will need dressing, so hold on and keep your head down. We don't want the Jerries using you for target practice.'

Both lads picked up the stretcher and made their way once again over the rough terrain, trying to keep the stretcher on an even keel. Colin nearly lost his balance but somehow managed to correct himself. A soldier from the trenches leapt out and made his way towards the two stretcher bearers.

'Here, let me help you. It's hard work for just the two of you.'

He took hold of one of the handles and helped Colin carry his side of the stretcher. Once at the trench they placed the injured man down. He was crying out in pain and they felt so hopeless.

'Let's get you to the advanced dressing station as soon as we can. The doctors there should be able to give you something for the pain. Then you will be transferred to the casualty clearing station. A surgeon will be able to operate on you.'

They dropped their seriously injured man at the advanced dressing station.

Bernard was there to instruct where the injured soldier should go, the worse the injury the more important it was to be seen as soon as possible by a doctor and operated on.

'Such terrible injuries. I'm not sure he will make it.' said Colin to Martin. 'We have done our best with what little equipment we have. He is in the best place for now.'

As promised, the two stretcher bearers made their way back to where they had left the other injured man.

'Right let's have a look at that leg wound. Looks to me as if the bullet has gone right through. Let's bandage it up and get you back to the safety of the trench. Hold on tight, lad, the going is a bit rough to say the least.'

It surprised both of them how brave these young men were, injured in the line of duty but keeping their dignity, being ever thankful for what help came their way.

After dropping the second man off at the dressing station, Martin looked at Colin and said, 'Right, I think it's time you and I got something to eat. Let's go and see what they are serving up today.'

Field kitchens were set up not far from the trenches so hot food could be served up to the troops. The smell of bully beef and boiled cabbage wafted up from the nearby kitchen.

'How are you two getting on? You look a bit muddy, chaps!'

'Yes, we've had a busy morning and will change these dirty clothes when we knock off later today.' The meal was served on a tin plate and both men tucked in, enjoying the hot nourishing food. They knew that they were safe for now. They sat and smoked a cigarette each, savouring the moment.

In the distance they could hear an ambulance train coming to collect the injured troops.

'Let's hope the lads we have rescued this morning get safely away to the base hospitals.'

A shout was heard: 'Can we have help down here someone?'

The two men stood up and stretched their tired muscles. They were soon at the point where the shouting was coming from.

'A soldier has been shot in the face. We have sat him on some sandbags.'

The sight before the two men was horrific. The soldier sat looking completely dazed by it all. On the left hand side of his face there was a bloody hole where his cheek should have been.

'Let's have a better look at you. By lad, this looks a mess. Still, let's get a dressing on that and get you back to the safety of the hospitals.' Martin got out a clean dressing and Colin wound a wide bandage around the soldier's face and part of the man's head.

'Not too tight. There, we need to get you to the medical centre as soon as possible.' They gently moved the man onto the stretcher and lay him down as best they could.

'Excuse us, chaps.' shouted Martin as they passed a group of soldiers. One or two of the men looked away.

'There, but for the grace of God, go I!'

Once at the dressing station they took the injured man straight in.

'Over here,' shouted a doctor. 'Let's have a look at what you have here. Can you go outside and see if there is an ambulance about? We need to get this man straight to the nearest field hospital. They will be able to get him out or possibly operate on him there.'

Martin and Bernard went outside and noticed a horse and cart operating as an ambulance.

'We have a man with a serious face injury. Can you get him to the nearest field hospital as soon as possible please?'

'Yes, I have room for about four more. Bring him out and we will get him as comfortable as possible. Then if there are any more emergency cases I can take them as well.'

'Let us help you get them loaded. Then you can get on your way.'

'I'll go back and sort out any badly injured that are well enough to travel.' shouted Bernard.

Soon the ambulance was loaded and on its way, away from the dirt and the mud of the trenches, away from the noise and the chaos.

Away to safety!

Chapter Nine

Life in the Trenches

Huddled together in the mud, wet and cold, was awful and terrifying for the new soldiers on trench duty.

Their morning started at 5.00 am, when they had to stand-to-arms for the sergeant to count his men and make sure they were up for the job in hand. They were given a tot of rum to temporarily warm them up and to give them a touch of Dutch courage. At 7.00 am breakfast was served: bread, bacon, and a cup of tea — hot if you were lucky, but mostly lukewarm. Over breakfast the men chattered about how they were feeling. One or two attempted to make jokes to cheer each other up.

'Are you alright, chap? You look a bit peaky this morning.'

William tried to smile but was feeling quite ill. It was hard for him to explain how he was feeling. He felt sick and giddy, his head ached, and he felt so miserable.

'What a night! The gun fire was so loud and the bright lights from exploding bombs were something else. Poor old Frank was hit in the side of his head. He lost an ear. Did you hear his scream? The stretcher bearers soon had him bandaged up and taken to the advance dressing station. My ears are still buzzing from the loud bangs.'

The men's task in this confined space was to keep the trench tidy, which was not easy. Rats ran along the trenches and over the men when they tried to sleep. The duck boards lining the base of the trenches were covered in mud and dirty water and were always slippery.

'We must try and bury that dead German soldier, the smell is atrocious. Look at the mass of maggots on his stomach wound. No wonder the rats are so large around here, there is a constant supply of dead meat for them. They get more food than we do!'

'Yes, I hate it when they scuttle all over us when we try to sleep. We don't get a lot of sleep anyway with the constant noise but these little blighters make my skin crawl.'

Charlie looked down the periscope. 'Get your gas masks on, men!' he shouted. 'The Germans have just released a couple of canisters.' He watched as the yellow smoke drifted on the breeze towards their trench. 'Get out of the trench as fast as you can and run like hell towards that derelict village. Find shelter behind a wall.'

In a panic the men grabbed their gas masks; they were ill fitting devices and smelt of rubber.

William was violently sick. He was not coping at all. He burst into tears.

'Come on, mate, you'll be alright. Let's get out of this hell hole.' Thomas pushed his mate up and over the slippery side of the muddy trench and followed as quickly as he could. He noticed several men running across the field with them, but suddenly one man ran into a crater hole filled with muddy water and disappeared. Thomas noticed air bubbles appearing on the surface.

'Let's help him,' shouted William.

'No, it's too late, mate. If we go in there the same will happen to us.'

By now William was shaking and fell to the ground.

'Come on, mate,' encouraged Thomas. 'Let's run to that barn where we can get our breath back.' Both men hid behind a wall and were soon joined by four or five other men.

William was crying, a hollow ghastly howl and, try as he may, Thomas could not comfort the distraught soldier. All he could do was cuddle the broken man in his arms as if he were a grieving child.

When they arrived back in the trench, Thomas had a word with the sergeant. 'Sir, I'm really worried about William. He's in no fit state to fight with us any more. Look, he has diarrhoea and its squelching over his boots. He has no control of himself. When he's not crying he sits and stares into space with a vacant look on his face.'

'I will go and have a word with him. Could you set the stove up and make us all a cup of tea?'

Thomas lit the stove and soon had a cup of hot freshly made tea. He handed the tin mugs around to the tired men.

'We need to get William to the advanced dressing station so he can get cleaned up and assessed by a doctor. He seems to be suffering from some sort of psychosis. Looks to me as if he may be suffering from shell shock.

The term Shell Shock was first coined in 1915 by a Medical officer Charles Myers of the British Psychological Society.

We need to get him home and into hospital, possibly the Neatly in Southampton. Thomas, you take him. It'll be reassuring if he has someone he knows with him. Get him to safety; we will hold the fort here. Good luck!'

Thomas led a tearful William along the muddy trench. 'Come on, brave soldier,' he said reassuringly.

'I don't feel very brave,' said a tearful William.

William was left at the advanced dressing station, where he waited patiently for a doctor to examine him. A kindly nurse helped him out of his dirty clothing and washed him as best she could. He was sent by ambulance train to Le Havre, then by hospital ship to Britain.

William's life became worse than a nightmare, reliving attacks, seeing the blood and gore, and hearing the terrifying noises during the long winter nights. He found it hard to swallow so eating became difficult. In his worst nightmares he went over the events where he bayoneted a German soldier. He heard again the blood curdling noise as the blood shot out of the middle aged man's mouth, hitting William's boots; the lifeless body lay in the dirt. William was physically sick when he realised what he had done. He had turned and run back to the safety of the British trench.

'I know it's difficult, lad,' said an understanding doctor, 'but he would have killed you had you not struck first. It's hard, but it's your job as a soldier. None of us were taught how to kill people in school and it's not in our nature to do so. Most of us were brought up in the church, learning how to love one another and to love God. With prayer, God will forgive you and you must learn to forgive yourself. Try to read one or two books. Hopefully it will help take your mind off the things.'

William was unable to concentrate on the world around him in the safety of this hospital, let alone read a book. He smiled weakly and lay curled up on his bed. How he so wished this was not going on, that he had never gone forward and volunteered. Would this horror ever leave him? But he must try to come out of the dismal dark place he was in. It went through his mind that he would be better off dead, like that poor German soldier. This wasn't living as he'd lived before the war. This was a living nightmare.

Back at the trench conditions had not improved.

Still it rained and the mud became thicker, the cold conditions for the soldiers became almost unbearable. They huddled up together during the night for warmth. But the body lice multiplied, they laid their eggs in the seams of the men's uniforms so the following morning they had to remove their jackets despite the cold and run the seams over a naked flame to burn the damn things. Squashing them with your nails was also a slow way to kill them. The trouble with the lice and the constant scratching was that bacteria could enter the men's skin and cause 'Trench Fever', symptoms of which were fever, headache, sore muscles and aching joints.

The soldiers would often find dogs from the local villages that had been abandoned when the occupants had left. This was good for the men's morale as they had something to stroke, and, if they were lucky and had a terrier dog, would attack and kill many of the rats. The men would sometimes shoot the rats but this was classed as a waste of a bullet. It was almost impossible to bury the dead as soon as they died - It was dangerous to climb out of the trenches to dig graves. Many of the bodies were covered up with mud as best as they could be.

Chapter Ten

<u>Hard Work takes its Toll</u>

During the summer of 1916 the medical profession was extremely busy due to the Battle of the Somme.

The first day of this battle was the bloodiest and remains the worst day in the British Army's history. British casualties on this first day were 57,470, of which a staggering 19,240 died. The battle lasted 141 days from July 1st to November 19th.

During this Battle the troops were living in extremely squalid conditions,. This, along with harsh winter weather and dwindling supplies, brought the Battle of the Somme to its end.

Len and Stanley were working all hours. It was not unusual for them to be woken at 4.00 am to find they were at the Casualty Clearing Station at Vecquemont Station. Len had been woken up and had a' wash and brush up.' This was one of his favourite sayings throughout his diary. We must assume he had a wash and got dressed ready for what his day had in store for him. Len was told to work as best as he could with one man down as Stanley had sprained his wrist.

The Vecquemont Railway Station was crowded as Len opened his carriage door and looked out at the mass of humanity. Stretcher bearers with badly injured men stretched out as far as the eye could see. Doctors and nurses were still trying to attend to the more seriously wounded.

'Right' shouted Len at the top of his voice, 'let's have the stretcher cases on first, I will show you where to put your patients.'

With that the first stretcher bearers hurled their stretchers up and onto the train; groans could be heard from the injured men as they were jostled about. The upper tier was loaded first which proved quite a job for the men as they gently lifted their patients off the stretcher into the top bunk. But with their expertise the top tier was soon filled, then the middle tier and lastly the bottom until the ward was full. It was Len's job, with the help of another orderly, to make the injured soldiers comfortable, covering them in clean white sheets and brown army issue blankets. At times this proved to be a difficult task with some of the more injured men, but Len was used to all this, so with reassuring words and gentle handling he soon had the men in his care as comfortable as possible.

That morning ambulance train number six took on a record load of 856 patients including several Leicesters. The Leicesters 678 and 9 went over the previous night.

Once the train was loaded the guard blew his whistle and waved his flag and the great steam train moved slowly away from the station. The train driver knew he had a special job to do and what a difficult journey this would be for the more seriously injured men.

It was now Len's job to prepare breakfast for the lads who were well enough to eat. He buttered the top of the unsliced loaf of bread then, with a very sharp knife, cut a thin slice off to go with the bacon which was now cooking. Breakfast was served about 10.30 am. By now the train was travelling at a good speed.

They arrived at Boulogne about 1.30 pm. Unloading the troops had to be well organised but the stretcher bearers waiting in turn on Boulogne Railway Station were now very efficient at their work and within two hours the train was almost empty and the injured solders were on their way to the base hospital.

For Len and Stanley the hard work continued - the linen had to be changed again and put into large linen boxes to go to be laundered. The blankets had to be sorted, some were folded and left at the end of the beds, but some were bloodied and dirty and covered in lice. These needed to be fumigated. The beds were wiped down with disinfectant, ready for the next influx of injured men. Then the floors needed to be washed down. Once all this was done the clean sheets arrived for the bunk beds to be made up again. Len wiped the perspiration from his brow; there was never quite enough room in this hospital ward railway carriage.

At 4.00pm,12 hours since Len's day had begun, he and Stanley knocked off to have a hot cup of tea. Both men needed to get washed and changed as their white coats were now grubby and soiled.

While in the staff canteen the 'Mails' were given out. Len was so excited as his bundle of mail was presented to him; he had a letter from his Mother, one from Cath, his sweetheart, a letter and a parcel from his Aunt Polly May and three postcards from some of his male friends. He neatly untied his brown paper package, putting the string into his trouser pocket. He never wasted anything and knew it could come in useful. His neat package contained chocolate and my, how Len loved chocolate! There were two packs of jellies plus three home-made fruit cakes.

Len suddenly noticed John. He was beaming from ear to ear as he walked towards his best pal. 'My you look happy, how are things going?'

'Len you will never guess, but I've found myself a girlfriend; her name is Monique. She is one of the French nurses in the field hospital where I have recently been working. We have been for walks when things quieten down in the evenings, out into the countryside.'

'Well, you dark horse, you,' said Len as he hugged his friend.

'I know its early days but I do love her, Len. I've never felt like this about anyone before.'

'It certainly suits you, this 'being in love' business.'

'Yes I can't wait to get to work in the mornings and sometimes when we have to work until really late I never mind any more.'

'Lad, I'm really pleased to see you looking so well and happy. Who would have thought, all those months ago when we walked over the fields in Woodhouse Eaves and you were undecided whether to sign up or not, you would be where you are today. I must get back to the train but let's hope we catch up again soon.' With one last hug the two friends parted.

Before the train left Boulogne for Abbeville, they were just about finished loading when a German aeroplane came over and dropped a couple of bombs, the second one dropping about 50–60 yards away from the end of the train. That seemed to put the wind up the driver and he started off very quickly. After the immediate shock of that episode, it was nice to have a fairly safe journey for a change.

Stanley arrived with his arm in a sling and a bandage round his sprained wrist.

'What have you been up to?' enquired Len.

'I fell and caught it in the metal railings round the bottom bunk bed on the last trip,' said a sorrowful Stanley.

'Trust you to be inactive on one of our busiest runs,' said Len, smiling and making a 'tut tut' noise.

The two friends sat enjoying a cup of cocoa that Len had made.

They arrived at Abbeville at about 8.30 pm. and received orders to proceed to Pouchvilles, which was well the other side of Doullovre so the train was not expected to reach there until the early hours.

'Right Stan, I've come over all tired so I'm going to retire. It's been a very long day. See you in the morning.' With that Len went and got ready for bed and finished the day writing in his diary.

Unfortunately Len had only had a few hours' sleep when he was called up and told to light up. As ordered, he went round and lit the oil lamps and prepared everything for more patients, only to be told to put the lights out again, so a very tired Len made his way back to bed.

Len woke with a start. He had been in a deep sleep after such a busy day yesterday, but, oh dear, he did not feel very well at all. His head ached, he had a sore throat and somehow he had to get up and get on. On standing up, the room went into a spin so he sat down on the bed. He managed to get down to the canteen but only managed a cup of tea.

'What's up mate?' asked a worried Stanley.

'I'm not too sure Stan, but I feel pretty rough.'

'Go back to bed and I will see if I can get one of the doctors to come and have a look at you.'

Len didn't need telling twice. After drinking his cup of tea he made his way back to the train and lay on his bed, still dressed in his uniform. Half an hour later there was a knock on his door.

'Come in,' whispered Len.

Dr Cunningham entered the small room and sat on a chair next to Len's bed. 'Right let's have a look at you,' the doctor said. 'You certainly feel hot to the touch. Let's have a look at your throat. Well, lad, it looks to me as If you have a nasty case of tonsillitis, which can unfortunately make you feel very poorly. I will leave these tablets; take one every four hours and try to drink plenty. If you feel no better in twenty four hours we will have to review the situation. I'd get into bed and try to sleep. Sleep is one of the best remedies when you're not feeling well. '

Once back in bed Len was soon fast asleep. Stanley looked in on his mate a couple of times. He would have to leave Len back at the barracks and get Robert to help him with the next train journey.

Len eventually woke up, not feeling much better. Stanley helped him to get down to the barracks and Len got back into bed and slept until morning.

By the morning Stanley was nowhere to be found. Both he and Robert had gone on the early morning train to pick up more injured soldiers. There was a job to be done and, with one man down, the trip would not be easy.

Len got up still feeling pretty rough. He went to the canteen to get another cup of tea. After drinking his tea he went in search of the doctor.

'My lad, you're not looking much better. How do you feel?'

'Still fairly poorly. I ache all over this morning; it feels like flu.'

'I'm wondering whether you have a touch of trench fever. I think you had better have a couple of days in the base hospital where the nurses can keep an eye on you.'

'I'm really sorry!' said Len. 'I really don't want to be a nuisance.'

'You're not being a nuisance, lad. You can't look after our troops if you're not well yourself. Go and get your night clothes and wash bag and bring your book if you are reading one.'

Len made his way back to the barracks, collected his few belongings and waited for a field ambulance to transfer him to the nearest base hospital.

As he entered the ward one of the VAD nurses recognised Len.

'Well, fancy seeing you here as a patient and not working,' said Emily as she smiled at him. 'There's a bed over there away from all the noise and bustle. You get yourself into bed and I will come and see you in a few minutes.'

Len gave a weak smile, how he didn't like being a patient. Trust him to get something to make him feel this poorly.

After a week of medicine and care from the nursing staff Len was still feeling no better.

'The trouble is, lad, you are going to feel weak for a few weeks so I'm going to send you to Poperinge, where you will stay in Talbot House. It was set up last year and it's where you can go to recuperate. You will be with other people getting over illness or injuries. There is good food, good company and a Chapel in the attic called 'The Upper Room.' Two weeks there and you should be well enough to report for duty. Poperinge is about eight miles from Ypres. There have been a lot of battles over there but you should be safe. Just take care, my boy, and have a good journey.'

'Thank you, Doctor. I really appreciate all you have done for me,' said Len.

The doctor turned away and went over to talk to another patient. Len lay back on his pillows.

The VAD Nurse Emily arrived at Len's bedside with a hot drink for him.

'Drink this and I will sort out some clothes for you, I will be back in about an hour.' Len smiled at this attractive nurse - she reminded him of his sweetheart, Cath, back in Leicester.

When Len was dressed he was ready to make his way to the railway station. One or two other men were going with him. He felt safer having company than having to travel on his own.

The railway station was fairly busy. The ambulance train on platform two had just unloaded its sick and injured men. Horse-drawn ambulances and motor ambulances waited outside.

'Come on lad' said one of the soldiers, 'let's get on this carriage - it's mostly for sitting cases'. The three men made themselves comfortable.

'You okay in there?' asked a friendly orderly.

'Yes, thank you.'

'When we have the train fully loaded I will make you all a cup of tea. There are not many to take on board here. We expect the next stop to be busier.'

The train pulled out of the station and within twenty minutes the orderly had arrived with the drinks.

'When I'm well I work as an orderly on ambulance train number six,' said Len.

'Do you? It's quite a full-on job, isn't it?'

Len nodded.

'It will take us roughly an hour and a half to get to Ypres, so I suggest you sit back and enjoy the ride.'

The three men sat back. Len had a lie down as he still felt rather tired if he exerted himself. Soon he had drifted off to sleep.

Chapter Eleven

<u>Talbot House</u>

Once again the railway station was busy.

As the three men made their way to the nearest exit, they noticed a Padre in his uniform with a white dog collar visible under his jacket. He was standing on a soap box, trying to make his small stature appear taller. He was the Reverend Geoffrey Studdart Kennedy. He had his Bible tucked neatly under his left arm as he encouraged the soldiers to march for their Lord. Several men stood around him and every now and again he would give them a blessing as he placed his hand on their shoulder and smiled warmly. He also handed out copies of the New Testament to the eager men.

He kept a supply of Woodbine cigarettes in his pocket which he gave to the lads. This earned the nickname of 'Woodbine Willie.'

Len felt compelled to go and have a word with him.

'How are you, young man?' asked the Padre.

'I'm on my way to Poperinge to stay at Talbot House. Unfortunately I've been unwell and I've been sent there by the doctor.'

'You will get on fine. It's such an inspirational place. My colleague, Rev Tubby Clayton, set the place up last year and everyone is treated the same, whatever their rank. You will have fine food, good company, and spiritual guidance.'

Len smiled as the Padre put an arm around his shoulder and blessed him.

'Here; take this New Testament with you and read about our Lord's ministry.'

Within an hour the three men had arrived at Talbot House. They were met at the door by a friendly cheerful Padre. It was Rev Tubby Clayton himself.

'Well, hello. We were expecting you. Come this way.'

He led the three men to the kitchen; there was a large oblong table in the middle of the floor.

'This is where we have our meals and the copper is always lit for hot water for a cup of tea or coffee, whichever you prefer. Let me take you upstairs and show you where you'll be sleeping.'

They were shown into a large bedroom set out with ten beds.

'The three down the left hand side are vacant at the moment so make yourselves at home. Once you have unpacked come back down to the kitchen and we will have a hot drink. Then I will show you the rest of the house.'

Within half-an-hour the three men were settled in the lounge. Len had found a book in the library and was sitting reading; the other two were reading newspapers.

Four uniformed men entered the lounge.

'Hello, chaps, it's good to see you. Are you our new recruits?'

'Yes we are,' said Len 'Here to recuperate.'

'Well you couldn't have come to a better place. You will soon feel well enough to take on the world. Dinner will be ready about 6.00 pm, so excuse us while we go and get changed.'

Len was feeling tired so made his way upstairs. He was soon fast asleep. He woke up when the dinner bell echoed round the entrance hall.

Sunday was a very busy day at Talbot House. Padres helping near the front line came to help with the Church of England services. Troops also came from near and far to attend these popular events. The first early service was at 8.30 am. They were held upstairs in an attic room that had previously been used for drying hops. This room was called 'The Upper Room' by all who gathered there. Men sat on the stairs once the room was full. The singing could be heard down the village streets. Many of the men prayed for friends and family; others prayed for peace and an end to the war; others gave thanks for being alive and prayed for injured friends. Tubby Clayton always gave an interesting sermon — one the troops could relate to.

Tea coffee and cake was served after these services and on fine days the men would sit outside in the garden.

While Len was recuperating at Talbot House the news filtered through that Bernard had been killed by shrapnel which had exploded when he was attending a wounded soldier, Bernard threw himself across the wounded man and had taken the full force of the blast, saving the soldier's life but losing his. Len was extremely upset on hearing this sad news, but also realised that Bernard's girlfriend, Freda, would be devastated. He sat down that evening and wrote a letter home to her, saying that Bernard had been so brave and had saved a soldier's life.

One Sunday afternoon, the Reverend Dougie Dennis sat in the lounge. Dougie was a tall, large-built man with blonde hair. He had a kindly way with him. He had blue eyes, a young complexion and dimples in his cheeks when he smiled. The men had taken to him almost as soon as they had met him.

In his soft voice he addressed the men. 'Right, men, I know a lot of you have sweethearts at home. Well,' he said with a pause, 'may I suggest that, on your next leave home, you consider marrying these girls.'

Dougie knew that many of the men would not survive the war, so to have some happy time at home would be very important. Dougie himself had been married to Anne for nearly two years and he couldn't be happier. The men really liked this idea and said yes, they would certainly think about it.

One evening Len went outside for some fresh air he wrapped his coat around him to keep out the cold. As he looked over to the church he noticed the lone figure of the Padre locking the church door.

'How are things going, Padre?' asked Len gently.

'Not too bad, lad. It's been a long day. But the Lord will guide us.'

'It's never easy though, is it Padre? We have a bad enough job caring for our injured men, but you have to stay strong when all around us is mayhem and chaos.'

'Yes. I was prepared for this job at home but never realised how difficult it could get. I'm ready for a good night's sleep, but I'm never too busy to help and listen to you soldiers.'

'Thank you, Padre. Goodnight.'

'Goodnight lad. Take care.'

Padres were kept extremely busy during the First World War. They comforted both patients and staff in the busy hospitals. They took so many funerals that some days they felt that was all they did.

One of the most difficult tasks for WW1 Padres was comforting the deserters; these scared soldiers were absolutely terrified so the thought of being shot at dawn by your own side was the most dreadful situation to find themselves in. It was almost impossible to comfort these frightened men who were to be shot for cowardice. It was more than being a coward; it was an absolute, genuine fear of what they had experienced - they could not cope with the trauma all around them.

Some of the men were suffering from shell shock. Many soldiers and Officers committed suicide. But these men, classed as deserters, had escaped not knowing where to, just a desperate need to get away. The fear when these men were eventually caught was paramount; they were not comforted or understood, just placed in isolation until the fateful morning when they were shot at dawn by British soldiers. The Padre was the only person who was allowed to spend the night in the prison cell trying to comfort them. He prayed with them; he reminded them that Christ had given his life too. He tried to read reassuring words from the Bible.

British and Commonwealth Military Command executed 309 of its own during the Great War.

It wasn't until 2016, a hundred years after our troops were being shot for desertion, that a "Posthumous Pardon" was granted for all of the 309 men.

The **Shot at Dawn Memorial** is a monument at the National Memorial Arboretum near Alrewas in Staffordshire, set up to honour and remember those unfortunate men. The Memorial is a sculpted concrete statue that portrays a young British soldier blindfold and tied to a stake, ready to be shot by a firing squad. The memorial was modelled on the likeness of 17 year old Private Herbert Burden who lied about his age to enlist in the armed forces. It is surrounded by a semicircle of stakes; on each is the name of an executed soldier.

After these events the Padre felt drained. He too needed words of comfort, but they seldom came.

Sunday services were always popular with the soldiers. They would come from near and far where possible to attend. It was a chance to get away from the horror of the front line. It felt safe to be in the barracks or the local church or in the Upper Room in Talbot house. It reminded the men of family at home as they sang the familiar hymns together and heard the readings from the Bible. The sermon was always interesting despite, on occasion, being rather long.

The job of the Padre was keeping up morale of the soldiers. They organised sport, cricket being extremely popular during the summer months. Len liked to score and write them in his diary. Football was also popular with the ambulance train staff; they would meet up with staff from the casualty clearing stations. It was a chance to meet other men from various regiments, to get to know them and enjoy time their time together. There was tea and biscuits to follow, which always went down well.

The YMCA (Young Men's Christian Association) would put on concerts for the men. Men would dress up as women and make the audience howl with laughter. French girls would sing to the men and the men were encouraged to sing along. All in all, a great night's entertainment was enjoyed.

Talbot House became known as Toc H. Toc H was set up by the Rev Philip Byard (Chubby) Clayton and, from its humble beginnings in WW1, is now an international Christian and charity movement.

Chapter Twelve

Ambulance Train Upgrade

This morning the train was at a standstill so Len and Stanley decided to have a look around the railway station. They went into the waiting room but found it rather busy with French passengers who smiled warmly at the soldiers.

'I know, let's go over to the canteen. I could just eat a rasher or two of bacon with a slice of toast and a cup of tea.'

As the men waited patiently, a friendly sergeant came up to them. 'Are you the boys from ambulance train number six?'

'Yep, that's us,' answered Len.

'Right, well let me introduce you — this is Percy, Percy Gloyne. He is from Yorkshire he is one of our engineers. He's hoping to do some work on your train while it's in the siding. They are planning to bring it up to date, so to speak.'

Percy was small in stature with a balding head. He had green eyes and a rather wispy moustache. He smiled at the men before him as he shook them by the hand. He spoke with a typical Yorkshire accent.

'I'm Len and this is my partner in crime, Stanley.'

Stanley nodded as he shook Percy by the hand.

'We work as orderlies on our ambulance train, and my, have we had some busy nights.'

'I've come to do some work on your train. Within a few weeks I will be able to supply the train with hot water and heating. You will certainly need it in these cold winters out here. It should make your life a lot easier. This is my right hand man, Wesley, who will assist me.'

Wesley held out his hand and shook each man's hand in turn. Wesley was older than Percy. He was tall with grey hair and a grey beard and moustache. His skin was dark and he had many wrinkles around both eyes.

'We have been doing some work in the trenches,' said Wesley. 'Trying to make them safer. With all of this wet weather the sides can collapse in on the men. It can be very frightening being half buried by wet heavy soil. We also dug out areas for the men to rest. We used corrugated iron to support the roof and sides, it has made it safer. It was hard but rewarding work. They now have places to go to play cards or chess or to read.'

'Right, men, let's go and get some refreshments, shall we?'

Percy and Wesley nodded and all four men went into the canteen. By this time there was no queue so they were able to get served quite quickly.

'So, whereabouts in Yorkshire are you from, Percy?' asked Stanley. 'My mother originated from Yorkshire, from Whitby.'

'Ah, yes a lovely quaint seaside town. Well I met my wife Mary at Risborough Hall just outside of Thornton- le-Dale.'

' Yes I know Thornton-le –Dale.'

'I have a young daughter, Agnes. She is two years old. We live in Wakefield. I'm a plumber by trade so joined the Royal Engineers. I can turn my hand to most things. Not very clever with the old sums and writing but give me something that needs fixing and I'm your man.'

'Our ambulance train is a French train, but do you know, Percy and Wesley, the first trains they used in 1914 were nothing more than old cattle wagons. They were used to transport horses from the ports to the front line, so on their way back they would carry wounded soldiers. There was no time to clean the wagons so the men were put on the dirty straw, their wounds open to infection. It was only when a group of nurses discovered what was happening that they set up a basic medical centre in the railway station. They tended the men's wounds, put on clean dressings, got local people to supply any spare mattresses and the wagons became more comfortable for the men to travel in. The men were on the trains for several hours at a time so something drastic needed to be done.'

'How interesting,' said Percy. 'We knew ambulance trains out here were pretty basic but those conditions were dreadful. We have ambulance trains that carry the sick and wounded back in England. And some of our British trains have already been sent out to France.'

'Yes, they are so much better than our French trains out here. I saw one last week and they have corridors, bigger ward cars.'

'We have also been instructed to install fans in your carriages — firstly to help the men who have been involved in gas attacks, and secondly to keep you all cool in the summer. In fact, a couple of weeks ago we fitted a lift in one of the hospital barges. They are extremely large inside and what a great way to travel, so slow and peaceful. Of course, they are not allowed to travel during the night so the journey takes twice as long, but the nursing staff are very dedicated.'

'That's interesting. We see them about from time to time but I've never been on one. I'm not sure how we would cope without our nursing staff.'

'Well now we have finished eating, we'd better take you to see our train.'

The four men left the canteen and made their way to the siding where ambulance train number six was stationary.

'Here we are,' announced a proud Stanley. 'Let us show you around.'

'We are expecting our tools and equipment to arrive later on today so that we can make a start while she is in this siding.'

'We need to clean the brasses and windows and any other jobs that need doing so we will make a start on that and catch up with you later,' said Len.

A couple of days later Len and Stanley were back in Rouen. Len went to look for John and Stanley went to the canteen for something to eat.

On finding John his mood was still buoyant. 'Len, I'm going to ask Monique to marry me. I would like to stay out here in France. After the War I can train here to become a nurse.'

'But hold on, John. What about your mother?' said Len as he held up his hand.

'Don't worry, Len. I've thought about that. I shall go home when I can and explain everything to her, then she can decide to stay in Woodhouse Eaves, or come to France and live with us.'

'My, you have certainly got it all worked out John.' said Len.

So my story ends. John went home to Woodhouse Eaves to tell his Mother his exciting news.

<u>WORLD WAR 1</u> came to an end at 11 am on Monday 11th November 1918.

It had started on Tuesday 28th July 1914.

Many troops spent time in France clearing up the dreadful mess of four years of fighting. It was a War worse than any other in recorded history.
Many of those young men, some under age, who so willingly signed up in 1914, 15 and 16, met with horrors beyond imagination.

In my story, John survived the War. He eventually moved to France and married Monique. He trained to be a nurse and they worked together in the same hospital.

Two years after the War was over, Stanley arrived back in Liverpool. It felt strange to be back in Britain, but how things had changed. There were no jobs, the women of the town had kept industry going and seemed rather reluctant to go home and go back to being housewives again. They were used to being out at work earning their own money.

But within three months Stanley had found himself a job at the docks. He enjoyed the hard work and the fact he was outside working near the water and fresh air of the River Mersey alongside other men who had been out in France during the War. Here the men could talk about army life without upsetting anyone. Stanley never married. He rented a small flat near the dockside and was quite happy to spend his evenings in the local pub.

Chapter Thirteen

Convalescent Home

Beaumanor, Woodhouse.

In Leicestershire, life had not stood still. Beaumanor in Woodhouse had been set up by Lord and Lady Greyson as a convalescent home to care for the injured service men. John's mother was working as a general help, washing and shaving the men and serving up meals and helping to feed them.

Beatrice also spent time at the Manor House. She would sit and read to the men and would also write letters home for them.

There was a very relaxed atmosphere. The views from the house were over the Leicestershire countryside. A lake at the bottom of the garden attracted dragon flies, butterflies, moths and bats. Frogs and toads made croaking noises as they made their mating calls to each other. A couple of swans had a large nest with five cygnets.

Beatrice sat outside with an injured soldier sitting either side of her. Harry was blind but his hearing was incredible.

'What bird is that I hear?' he asked.

'It's a skylark; she has a nest on the ground in the field beyond the fence of the garden. She flies so high, it's really difficult to see her, but her song must be one of the sweetest song birds there is.'

The three people sat quietly enjoying the warmth of the spring sunshine on their faces.

'I still hear the sound of the battles, the explosions, and the cry of the wounded men, then the long silence. I still suffer from buzzing in my ears.'

'You are safe now' reassured Beatrice as she held the soldiers hand 'with time these memories will fade.'

She noticed tears in Harry's eyes.

'Over on the fence is a male bullfinch feeding his baby from the insects on the honeysuckle' whispered Beatrice. She described the bird to Harry 'He has a deep pink chest and black markings on his head.'

'Yes, I can see him,' said William, who sat on the other side of Beatrice. 'Nature is so wonderful. I often hear an owl hoot when I'm trying to get to sleep; they sound so haunting, like a ghost in the shadows.'

Agnes Greyson walked down the steps with a tray of drinks for everyone. 'Cook made these scones this morning,' she said as she placed the tray on the small garden table.

'How are you this morning, boys?' she asked in her gentle manner.

'We are enjoying this sunshine and we cannot thank you enough for your hospitality. The clean sheets and comfortable beds are so different from the wet muddy clothes complete with lice. The lice seemed to eat us alive; we itched so much that scratching made our skin very sore.'

'You are safe here.' said Agnes as she put her hand reassuringly on Harry's shoulder. Harry smiled but felt so unsure what the future held for him.

Harry felt a cold wet nose on his hand.

'Hello, boy' he said to Rover - Lord Greyson's Golden Labrador. Harry stroked the dog's warm ears and Rover nuzzled even closer to the blind man. 'He has such a soft coat and is very friendly.' Harry bent down to kiss the top of the dogs head. 'He seems to sense you cannot see as he always comes up close to you.'

'I tell you what, Harry. We have some new born kittens in the stables. Why don't you get Beatrice to write home to your parents to see you if you can have one? If you start looking after it now while it's a kitten it will be used to you by the time you go home' said Agnes.

Harry smiled. 'Yes, thank you. What a good idea; it will take my mind off of my own problems and let me focus on something else. I'm pretty sure my parents will approve of the idea. We had cats when I was a child.'

'Harry, here is a letter for you.' said Agnes 'I'm sure Beatrice will read it to you.'

She passed the unopened letter to Harry who passed it to Beatrice.

'Dear Harry, we are so sorry to hear that you have lost your sight, dear boy, but at the same time so relieved that you are alive. We are pleased to say you are now an uncle - your sister Joyce has had a daughter and named her Victoria after our late Queen. You will be able to hold her in your arms as soon as you return home to us. We look forward to seeing you soon. Much love Mother and Father.'

'Yes it will be nice to go home but what will become of me? I'm no use to anyone like this - a poor bloody blind man.'

'Harry you are a good-looking man. I'm sure in the future you will meet a girl and get married. And if you have your kitten to look after that will be good. Let us go back inside, it becomes quite cold when the sun goes behind a cloud.'

Back in the Manor House Dr Greyson was doing his rounds. He sat on the edge of the men's beds and talked to his patients. Those well enough to be out of bed sat in the lounge playing cards or reading, a couple of men were in deep concentration over a game of chess.

Agnes came in from the stables with a small black and white kitten in her arms.

'Here you are, Harry. You will have to think of a name for him.'

She placed the small fluffy bundle into Harry's arms. Harry's face lit up as he cuddled the tiny kitten.

'He's purring can you hear him?'. Harry sat for half an hour stroking his new acquaintance.

'It's time to get ready for the evening meal. Let me take him back to the stable. Have you decided what to call him?'

'Teddy,' said Harry, 'and I can shorten it to Ted. He's soft just like my old teddy was when I was a little boy.'

Beatrice smiled at Agnes; it was amazing how a small kitten could alter Harry's outlook on life.

After the evening meal the fire was lit in the lounge and most of the patients sat together talking. John's mum stayed well into the evening and sometimes stayed overnight when a patient needed extra care. She felt this such a worthwhile job and she loved it. She received a postcard from John telling her that he had met a French nurse called Monique. he was hoping to marry her after the war. She was delighted for her son but decided her life was complete here in Woodhouse Eaves. She would try to go over to France for the wedding but felt it only fair that she let them live their own lives.

Beatrice would mostly go home around four o'clock so she could cook the evening meal for her growing family. May was now helping her father, Ernest, in his shoe mercer business. Stanley was now at secondary school.

Beatrice also loved receiving cards and letters from Leonard. Although she knew they had been censored, she loved to see his neat writing and to learn that he was doing alright. She felt so proud of her eldest child.

Ernest still bought his newspaper from a vendor just outside Leicester railway station, although now it was a much older man selling them. He read the paper after his evening meal; he read about the War and the home news. He always kept his thoughts to himself; he still went outside to smoke his pipe. He knew that although his wife could read she never read the newspaper.

The whole Folwell family looked forward to Len coming home. When they could once again be a complete family unit.

But of course the War would change Len, the horrors he witnessed during his time in France would stay in his mind for a long time. But with the passing of time these thoughts would eventually become a distant memory.

He came home not only to his family but to his sweetheart, Cath. He had written to Cath throughout his time abroad. She had lived with her sister and worked in Leicester.

On the 8th September 1921 Len married his sweetheart, Cath. at The Congregational Chapel in Oxford Street, Leicester. Len was a 'Shoe Mercer' working for his father Ernest's business, supplying the lining for shoes to the busy Leicester shoe trade. His new wife, Elizabeth Catherine Browett, was a football bladder maker.

Cath was the youngest child of nine. She lost an elder brother, George Edward Browett, during the Great War.

He, like many, had run away from home to sign up. He died, aged 27 years, on Wednesday October 9th 1918 - one month before the war ended.

Len and Cath lived in Leicester, where their only child, a daughter called Joyce May, was born in 1930.

They moved to London where Len worked for Millet's - the outdoor store.

At the outbreak of World War II Len said, 'Not another bloody war. I've lived through one already. We were promised there would never be another War.

How wrong they all were.

Len moved back up to Leicestershire with his young family to live in the village of Billesdon.

Millet's was a Jewish company so Len was moved to Leicester for his family's safety.

He lived in Billesdon for many years, leaving his home every morning to get the bus into Leicester, dressed in his dark suit and bowler hat with his briefcase under his arm

During the Second World War, Len became Warden for the village of Billesdon. He went round the village after dark making sure people had their black out curtains over their windows.

There was a Prisoner of War Camp in Billesdon. For the first year or two it had Italian prisoners. It then had German prisoners of war. The German prisoners worked on local farms. They were allowed to walk around the village where many of the villagers invited them into their homes. My grandparents, Len and Cath, became friendly with several of the men. They went to Sunday services with them and had Sunday tea with them. Emile, one of the German prisoners, kept in touch with Cath and Len after the War. He always called Cath his 'English Mother.'

Len and Cath enjoyed being back in a village a few miles from where Cath had spent her childhood. Cath worked at a private school in the village which their daughter, Joyce, attended.

Chapter Fourteen

<u>LEICESTERSHIRE</u>

For anyone who knows Woodhouse Eaves in Leicestershire, you will know that the church and the Manor House are not in the same village. The church I describe is the church in Woodhouse Eaves but the Manor House is actually in the village of Woodhouse - roughly four miles away.

I discovered that the people of the Manor House did actually go horse riding with the Quorn Hunt during WW1. I also found that the winter of 1915 was cold and wet. But that does not sound as romantic as telling my reader

'It started to snow.'

The railway line and station are actually in Quorn, where the line linked Leicester to Loughborough and beyond. The old railway line is still there and the old steam trains still travel along the tracks, making it very nostalgic. The track stops abruptly on the outskirts of Leicester now, but travels to the old railway station in Loughborough.

At the beginning of 1916 the people of Woodhouse and Woodhouse Eaves and surrounding area heard a strange rumbling noise. It was discovered to be an earthquake under Bradgate Park.

Within a week another strange noise was heard. It was just after eight o'clock and the people at the Manor House were about to have their evening meal.

People left their homes to see if they could see what was happening.

A German Zeppelin had somehow crept up the middle of England during the night, making its ghostly whirring noise.

Most of the towns, including Leicester, were hidden under blackouts but Loughborough was not prepared. Her lights were shining out in the black night sky and she was bombed by the Zeppelin. The four bombs dropped made a terrific explosion; many of the buildings were damaged. The raid killed ten people and injured twelve.

This was about the same time that Len and John had sailed across to France.

I would like to thank Caroline Wessel for letting me use information from her book, Beaumanor - War and Peace.

Chapter Fifteen

<u>Netley Hospital</u>

The one place in the UK that experienced the horrors of WW1 first hand was the Netley Hospital near Southampton. Here the wounded were delivered, complete with mud from the trenches and their terrible injuries, by hospital ship then train.

This magnificent building was The Royal Victoria Military Hospital.

Queen Victoria laid the foundation stone on the 19th May 1856

The hospital eventually opened for patients on 11th March 1863.

It was the world's biggest hospital, built to serve an empire. It was a quarter of a mile long, had 138 wards and approximately 1,000 beds.

A railway line connected Netley to Southampton docks at the suggestion of Queen Victoria so she could visit.

The hospital was in use during the Second Boer War (1899—1902).

From its construction until 1902, Netley Hospital served as the home of the Army Medical School, training civilian doctors for service with the army.

During WW1 a large Red Cross hutted hospital was built at the rear of the site, which expanded Netley to accommodate around 2,500 beds. The vast area was as big as a town; it had its own gasworks, bakery, school, stables, reservoir and even a prison. There was a saltwater swimming pool, fed by a windmill pumping water from the sea. The kitchens supplied food that was more nutritious than the food on the Western Front.

Not only was it the largest building in England but was also known as 'The Largest Palace of Pain'.

Thousands of men and women lived there. Many of the staff were Red Cross volunteers. Young local girls with no previous medical experience had to deal with men without limbs or faces. Like John in our story, it took several weeks to adjust to the situation they found themselves in.

Some 50,000 patients were treated at Netley during WW1.

Netley had a special ward for soldiers with mental health problems, known during WW1 as 'Shell Shock'. It had a padded room where men could go for their own safety. It was about this time that they discovered hypnosis could help with this debilitating condition. At the end of the war, 80,000 people had suffered from 'shell shock' which is known today as Post Traumatic Stress Disorder. (PTSD).

Electric shock treatment was also in its early stages.

Psychiatrists discovered a gentle approach often helped these unfortunate soldiers. Talking therapy and being understood was a long way from being shut up in a lunatic institution in the early 1800's.

By 1918 there were 20 hospitals in Britain designated to care for the mentally ill.

Chapter Sixteen

Padre

The Padre played such an important part during The Great War.

Reverend Studdart Kennedy

The Reverend Geoffrey Anketell Studdart Kennedy was born in Leeds on 27th June 1883. His father was a clergyman and Geoffrey followed in his father's footsteps. Geoffrey trained at Ripon Clergy College in Yorkshire.

Geoffrey enjoyed working with the under privileged, giving them financial support and spiritual help. He also enjoyed open air preaching. This stood him in good stead for his work during World War 1.

Geoffrey became a Padre during The Great War and worked in and near the trenches, comforting men who were wounded and helping to get important medicine to them.

He became known as 'Woodbine Willie' as he always carried packets of Woodbine cigarettes, which he gave out to the troops along with copies of the New Testament.

Geoffrey wrote many poignant poems about his life during World War 1.

Geoffrey survived WW1 but unfortunately died at the age of 45.

Running Into No Man's Land is a book written about the life of Geoffrey's life by Jonathan Brant.

Reverend Theodore Bayley Hardy

Theodore Bayley Hardy was born on 20th October 1863 in Exeter.

Like Geoffrey, he started his working life as a school teacher. He was ordained in 1898.

Theodore was 51 years old when World War 1 started; he volunteered but was told he was too old. Eventually he was accepted and, in August 1916, went out to serve in France.

Theodore also enjoyed being with the men in the front line trenches. Many a night he would sit or lie next to a badly wounded soldier keeping him company until help arrived or the soldier died.

For his dedication the Reverend Theodore Hardy received three medals; the Victoria Cross, the Distinguished Service Order and the Military Cross.

Sadly, he was killed in action on 18th October 1918 in Rouen in France.

It's Only Me by David Raw is a book written about Theodore's life before and during WW1.

Reverend Dougie Dennis

Rev Dougie Dennis is a friend of mine and is a Padre who retired to the town of Melton Mowbray. He is a very well-liked and respected man.

Dougie was a Padre during the unrest in Northern Ireland.

Dougie was taught embroidery during a hospital stay in the Second World War.

My grandfather, Leonard also enjoyed doing embroidery.

Chapter Seventeen

<u>Percy Gloyne</u>

Percy Gloyne was my husband's grandfather. He was born on the 5th January 1881 to Frederick and Ellen Gloyne. Percy was the second eldest of six children.

When Percy left school he went into the plumbing trade.

Some work needed doing at Riseborough Hall which was a beautiful old stone building, part of which dated back to the 16th century. It stands on Riseborough Hill and commands sweeping views across Ryedale from its imposing position. It is just outside Thornton-le- Dale in North Yorkshire. .

While at the Hall Percy moved in with George and Eliza Fletcher, who lived in a tied cottage. George was a coachman and his wife Eliza was a housekeeper, Mary, their daughter, was a nanny to the children. Percy started courting Mary and they were married on Wednesday 22nd October 1913.

Mary and Percy subsequently moved back to Wakefield. They lived in a flat above a shop. Percy continued his plumbing work while Mary ran the shop.

On 12th January 1915 Mary and Percy had a baby daughter, Agnes Mary. (My husband's mother)

Percy served his country with the Royal Engineers during the First World War. He was killed on Wednesday 2nd May 1918 aged 38 years; he had been married to Mary for four and a half years.

We know from Percy and Mary's only daughter, Agnes Mary, who was only three years old when her father was killed, that Mary (her Mother) never remarried. She moved from Wakefield to be nearer her family and from there she moved to Scarborough, where she ran a guest house for several years.

When Percy and Mary's daughter Agnes was 80 years old, her son Christopher and daughter Elizabeth took her to Couin New British Cemetery in France to visit her father's grave. It was here she could say her final, 'Goodbye,' to him.

Chapter Eighteen

<u>The Western Times , Saturday 8th MAY 1915</u>

<u>LUSITANIA SUNK</u>

By German Pirate off Irish Coast

NO WARNING GIVEN

How Germans Carried Out Their Threat.

AMERICANS ABOARD

A Great Loss of Life Feared.

WIRELESS MESSAGE

"Come at Once: A Big List,"

RESCUE WORK

Between 500 and 600 Survivors Landed.

The news flashed over the wireless yesterday afternoon that the giant Cunard, the "Lusitania," sister ship to the Mauretania had been torpedoed and sunk by a German submarine eight miles off the Irish coast. Caused the deepest concern throughout England. The announcement of the outrage was, as soon as it became known, issued by the Press Bureau, but the bare fact of the sinking of the liner was sufficient to cause the Cunard offices at Liverpool to be besieged by hundreds of people who had friends and relatives on board the ill-fated Atlantic greyhound. The Cunard officials were unable to impart the needed information at so early an hour, as the facts had not been received up to six o'clock last evening as to how many had perished as the result of this latest diabolical outrage by the German submarine.

The" Lusitania" which for many years held the Atlantic record for the quickest passage from New York to Queenstown, but which was eventually taken from her by the "Mauretania" was regarded as one of the best and fastest liners afloat; in fact, she had been aptly described as a floating palace.

Many times she has appeared in the Western Port at Plymouth, and her well defined lines have been the admiration of all who were privileged to see her. And now she rests beneath the waves off the Irish coast, with it is feared, many brave souls who barely a week ago were probably wishing "Goodbye" to their dear ones at New York. Little did the passengers think when the "Lusitania" steamed out of New York harbour that in less than a week the grand Cunard would become a prey to that mode of warfare which has aroused the indignation –and justly so- of all the persons who have a spark of feeling left in them for that which is fair, just or honourable.

The sinking of the "Lusitania" by the German submarine has capped anything which the German pirates had previously attempted. It is a significant fact that prior to the Cunarder leaving New York the Germans openly avowed that they would, if opportunity arose, send her to the bottom, it also stated that American passengers were warned that they sailed in the "Lusitania" at their own risk.

The "Lusitania" was torpedoed and sunk at 2.33 yesterday afternoon, eight miles south by west of Kinsale, South of Ireland.

Chapter Nineteen

THE DERBY DAILY TELEGRAPH

MONDAY 24th MAY 1915

THE

Gretna Railway Disaster

Appalling Loss of Life,

DEATH ROLL MAY APPROACH 200

A GOODS TRAIN ALSO INVOLVED

HEARTRENDING SCENES.

The railway disaster which occurred on Saturday morning on the Caledonian line a short distance north of Gretna Green is the most appalling of its kind in the whole history of British railways. The earlier accounts were sufficient to have established this fact, but evidence was forthcoming on Sunday to show that the earlier estimate as to the loss of life was certainly trebled, and yet maybe quadrupled. The latest figures on Sunday night vary from 157 to nearly 200, with a list of injured on a corresponding scale.

The following description account is from the special correspondent on the spot of the "Daily News"------

The scene is an isolated place in the comparatively flat agricultural district immediately over the Scottish border, and within hail of the toll-house at Gretna Green, where runaway lovers went to seek hurried marriage at the hands of the blacksmith in the romantic days before a great main railway cut through the country. It is about half a mile beyond Gretna, at which point the Caledonia Railway and the North- Western Company's trains run over the Caledonia metals on going north into Scotland from Carlisle.

The place indicated just beyond Gretna is known as Quintinshill, where a signalman's cabin commands an immediate view of the main line.

About seven o'clock in the glorious spring of Saturday morning there was a goods train standing on the main line at Quintinshill. The 6.10 a.m. local passenger train from Carlisle, which left late on its northerly journey, arrived at this spot also. The Euston- Glasgow express was following. It was due to leave Carlisle at 6.05 but was even later than the local train, which, however, it was rapidly over taking. It was necessary, therefore, to divert the "local" to allow the express to pass, and as the goods train was in the up loop the slow passenger train was turned on the down main line.

It had hardly come to standstill when the troop train, packed with soldiers, hurtling at 50 miles an hour down the long slope from Beattock, crashed into it. It was the troop train that suffered most by the impact, but considerable parts of both trains were thrown on the up main line; and almost instantly the Euston-Glasgow "sleeper" one of giants of the railway, forging uphill under the power of two great engines, ploughing at nearly sixty miles an hour into the wreckage.   So substantial was the debris that lay in its track that the express came almost to a dead stop, hurling great pieces of wood and iron over hedges and ditches into the fields around.

The goods train was nearly buried, and its engine was derailed. Only one element was needed to make the already appalling disaster supremely and terribly complete. That fatal contribution came almost at once: fire burst through the shattered woodwork that was piled deep above the live massed and interlocked engines.

When fire began, any hope of rescue for scores pinned and mutilated passengers, slender enough in any case, vanished utterly. It is not easy to describe or even imagine the agonies of many who were not killed outright: their sufferings were ended only as the flames actually enveloped them.

Two factors relieved in some poor degree the colossal tragedy- the superhuman exertions of the rescuers and the heroism of the survivors and of those brave fellows who, with unspeakable courage, saw inevitable death advancing in the flame that spread so greedily in the hot, clear air, which hardly a breath of wind disturbed. Had death come upon them on the battlefield for which they were bound it could not have come more violently or with more horror. And no men could have met death with greater fortitude than those whose end came in the holocaust that raged amid such peaceful surroundings and on so perfect a spring day.

This was the worst Railway Disaster in the whole of British History.

Chapter Twenty

Evening Telegraph.

TUESDAY JUNE 6TH 1916.

LORD KITCHENER AND HIS STAFF PERISH.

Cruiser Sunk in the North Sea

Tragic End of War secretary.

The Secretary of the Admiralty announces the following telegram has been received from the Commander-in-chief this morning---

I HAVE TO REPORT WITH DEEP REGRET THE H.M.S. HAMPSHIRE CAPT. H. J. SAVILL, R. N. WITH LORD KITCHENER AND HIS STAFF ON BOARD WAS SUNK LAST NIGHT AT 8. P.M. TO THE WEST OF THE ORKNEYS EITHER BY MINE OR TORPEDO. FOUR BOATS WERE SEEN BY OBSERVERS ON SHORE TO LEAVE THE SHIP.

THE WIND WAS NORTH- NORTH- WEST, AND HEAVY SEAS WERE RUNNING.

PATROL VESSELS AND DESTROYERS AT ONCE PROCEEDED TO THE SPOT AND A PARTY WAS SENT ALONG THE COAST TO SEARCH, BUT ONLY SOME BODIES AND A CAPSIZED BOAT HAVE BEEN FOUND UP TO THE PRESENT AND THE WHOLE

SHORE HAS BEEN SEARCHED FROM THE
SEABOARD.

I GREATLY FEAR THAT THERE IS LITTLE HOPE OF
THERE BEING ANY SURVIVORS.

NO REPORT HAS YET BEEN RECEIVED FROM THE
SEARCH PARTIES. HIS MAJESTY'S SHIP WAS ON
HER WAY TO RUSSIA.

Empire's Greatest Military Organiser.

The tragic end of one of Britain's greatest soldiers will be
received with regret all over the British Empire.

Lord Kitchener has been constantly in the public eye; and
at the beginning of the present War the Empire looked to
him as the one man for the administrative helm.
"Kitchener at the War Office." had long been a national
aspiration.

He has been called the Empire's Greatest Military
Organiser.

LONDON'S SYMPATHY.

The Lord Mayor of London has sent the following
telegram to the Prime Minister---

The citizens of London have received with profound
distress the news of the death of Field-Marshal Earl
Kitchener, Secretary of State for War, himself a

distinguished citizen and places on record its sorrow that a career of immeasurable national service ever dedicated to the cause of his Sovereign and country, should have been close in this tragic manner. To yourself and your colleagues the City of London offers its sympathy and condolences.

Chapter Twenty One

<u>Leonard's Diary</u>

73552 Leonard Folwell.
R.A.M.C. (Royal Army Medical Corps)
No 6 Ambulance Train
France.

20th January 1916
Left Aldershot & embarked on the "Manchester Importer."
Steamer for France.
Voyage good but not sufficiently loaded & rolled rather
badly. Was sea sick & did picket on top of the stairs near
cabins from 12:22 to 2.00am.

21st January... Arrived off Le Havre & waited for the tide
until about 9.30am. Good voyage up the Seine & some
very good scenery. Landed at Rouen 7.45 pm. After
being on Boats 25 hours marched to the Base. Put into
tents & "Slept Like A Top."

22nd January Not much doing. Left to rest after the
journey. Concert at the Y.M.C.A. at night very decent.
Only allowed to write one letter per day & so wrote home.
Lights out in this camp 9.15 pm.
During day gave in my name as clerk & typist & hope job
will come off. That is the only branch of the Corps where I
could ?? Felt very jolly all day.

8th February 1916.
Was detailed for Ambulance Reinforcements.

9th February Left Rouen for Abbeville to be sent to a
train. Arrived in Abbeville at about 1.00am.

10th February   Got off Train at about 6.45 am. Hung
about Abbeville Junction for several hours & then was
detailed for Number 6 Ambulance Train. Left Abbeville at
2.7pm. To join unit.

The Train was resting.

Whilst at this garage spent time working on fatigues at nos.18 & 20 General Hospitals except for about 10 days at Nott General Hospital.

Routine for day:

Reveille 6.30 am. Parade for Roll Call, detailed to duties 7.00am. Breakfast 7.45am. Parade for fatigue duty at Hospitals 8.45am. Work at Hospital till 11.45am. Dinner 12.45 pm. Parade for 1.45pm. Work at Hospital till 3.45pm. Tea. 4.00pm. Lights out at 9.30pm.

Saturday 15th April 1916

Reveille 6.30 am. Got up at 6.45am.

On sanitary fatigue first thing. Breakfast 7.30 am Roasted cheese, bread, butter jam & tea.

On fatigue at nos 20 General Hospital 8.15am. Swept up road & cleared up paper, orange peel etc. from a piece of ground & then started to dig a pit with P. Bernard. Had a ?? with Lanky (Cpl) about time for finishing & couldn't agree. Anyway knocked off at 12.00 noon. Dinner 12.30pm. Bully Beef & Piccalilli, rice pudding & jam.

20th General Hospital again at 1.45pm.& set to scrub out a H Tent (Hospital Tent.) But Sargent in charge of job too windy, so did not get much done.

About 3.30pm. Sergeant came rushing into tent. ' Aren't you two (Holiday & Self) R.A.M.C. men? ' 'Yes!' 'Come along to bay office.' Found out that an officer had fell from his horse on the beach & we were to go down & fetch him up. No Ambulance to be found in the camp, so started out with wheeled stretcher .

Sunday 16th April

Reveille 6.30am.Got up at 6.55am. Parade 7.00am. Got

back & lay down till breakfast 7.30 am . Breakfast Bacon, bread, jam & tea.
Cleaned up coach & then sent onto K Coach, to clean brasses & panels & went for Medical inspection at 10.45am. At Medical Inspection until 11.30am. Lay down until dinner time. Dinner Roast beef, veg, (mixed) & potatoes. Lay down and read for about an hour after dinner & then went to see a Football match between 18 & 20 General Hospitals. Results 1 - 0 in favour of 18. Very exciting game. Tea, bread, butter, dripping, jam marmalade Tea. In the evening wrote three letters to Bert, Dickl ? ? & Cath (later to become his wife.) Had a bit of roasted cheese, bread, butter for supper & get down to it at 8.30pm.& lay reading until 9.15pm.& then put the lamp out & went to sleep.

Monday 17th April.
Reville 6.30am. Got up at 6.50am. Parade 7.00am Detailed for coach duty. Breakfast roasted cheese, bread, butter, tea.

Sunday 9th July. Romescamps (Abancourt)

Reveille 6.00 am. Got up at 6.15 am. Parade 6.30 am. Wash & brush up & go for breakfast about 7.00 am. Breakfast dried bacon, bread, tea. Cleaned brasses & panels of coach & went to the office re new pack knife. Had to sign two papers fir it, & then take a slip to Cpl Turphy in Q. Ms. Store to draw it there sign for it again. Back to the coach & washed the cross etc. on one side of coach & also floor boards & then went & cleaned up one side of one of the latrines Pay parade at 11.45 am. &

drew 5 francs. Dinner 12.15 Roast beef & potatoes. Cricket match arranged no's 9 train in afternoon promised to score for our side. Came back from dinner & started to put a pocket in my trousers.

2.00 pm. Parade. After Parade came & finished pocket. At 3.30 pm. Went across to see the match & score. Results of match 29 runs to 22 No 9 won by ?? Tea 5.00 pm. Bread, butter, jam & tea. After tea wrote two P C (post cards) one to Mother & one to both. Answered roll on guard at 6.30 pm for ?? then went to see a football match between some Tommie's & Frenchmen but didn't take much interest in the match as I met some L. T. 6 men who had got stranded & was talking to them. Got back to train about 9.30 pm but went over to the canteen around about 9.30 & had a cup of tea & some biscuits for supper. Back to train again & got down to it about 10.30 lay talking till about 11.30 then went to sleep.

Monday July 10th 1915 (wrong date.)

Romescamps was not knocked up & consequently overslept & rose at 6.40 am. Washed & brush up & went for breakfast about 7.15 am Breakfast dried bacon, bread, & tea. Back to coach & polished up brasses & panels & then went & washed crosses etc. on No. 1 kitchen.

Washed & shaved brushed up & went for dinner about 12.40 pm. Dinner Bully beef, piccalilli, potatoes & bread, also jam. Coach again & lay down reading till parade at

2.00 pm. Nothing doing during afternoon so had a lay down & started reading 'The Riddle of the Sands' by Erskine Childers. Tea at 4.00pm. Bread, butter, jam & tea. & I had some apricots which I had bought. After Tea messed about for a bit & then arranged a game of cricket with some R (Royal) Engineers, but we could only number nine a side. No 6 won by 26 runs to 24. Half past eight parade was late. Held about 8.45 pm. After parade had some roasted cheese, bread, butter, & tea for supper . down to it about 10.00pm. after learning that we were due to start for Vickersmont (Leonard's spelling of Vecquemont) at 12.8 am.

Tuesday July 11th Vickersmont.

On being awakened this morning at about 4.45 am. Found the train was at the C. C. S (Station) at Vickersmont (just past Amiens) Got up & had a wash & brush up & was told to stay in the coach to load as Stanley had a sprained wrist. Started loading train at about 5.99.am. Loaded up a record load. Took 856 patients had 8 in my coach. After loading went into the kitchen to cut up bread, butter & bacon & breakfast was served up at about 10.30 am. At Abbeville. Went on again to Boulogne. Arrived at Boulogne about 1.30 pm. Unloaded changed linen etc. by about 4.00 pm. Mails given out received letters from Mother, Cath, Aunty Polly May, Sgnt ??? Wakefield & Dick ??? a field PC from Bert & a parcel from Aunt Polly containing chocolate jellies cakes etc.& a cricket (match) ball which I wrote home for.

Went & had tea. Train left Boulogne at about 4.30 pm.
For Abbeville. Arrived there at about 8.30 pm. & received
orders to proceed to Pouchevilles. At once so came in
wrote diary & got down to it. Soon after leaving Abbeville,
Pouchevilles being well the other side of Doullovre.
Should not reach there until the small hours of tomorrow.
So shall try for a sleep. Was called at about 11.30pm. to
light up. Lit up & prepared for patients, but was told to put
lights out. So got down to it.

Wednesday July 12th Gourchelles.

Reveille about 6.00 am. Got up & went on parade at 6.30
am. Wash & brush up. Breakfast, fried cheese, bread,
butter, & tea at 7.00 am. Washed out coach. Dinner
12.30 pm. Roast beef, onion sauce, potatoes & bread.
Better than usual. Back to coach & reading till 2.00
parade. Back to coach again & slept till 4.15 pm. went &
had tea, bread, butter, dripping, jam & tea. Back to coach
& wrote letters home & to Cath. About 6.30 pm. Went into
village & had a look round, not a bad village as French
villages go.

Back to train about 8.45 pm. Parade 8.30 pm. into coach
again & had some fried cheese & bread for supper. Went
& fetched some water & came back & wrote a letter to
Aunt Polly. Wrote diary & am now going to bed 9.30 pm.
Have been expecting to load up all day but we are still

here & no sign of loading up tonight.

Thursday July 13th   Pouchevillers.

Reveille 6.00 am. Got up at 6.15 am. Parade 6.30 am.
Back again had a wash & brush up & went for breakfast
at 7.00 am. Fried bacon, bread, butter, tea. Cleaned up in
coach & polished some of the brasses & started loading
quite a small. Load. Only about 250 patients only 23 in
my coach all stretcher cases. Served up dinner at about
7.00 pm.& got washed up & the beds tidied & was able to
sit down for about half an hour. Tea up about 4.00 pm.
Got this served up & the pots washed & arrived in
Abbeville at about 5.20 pm. Stayed about 30 – 40
minutes & got mails up. Received a letter from Mother &
one from Edna.

Started off again from Abbeville & I cleaned up the tea
pail & had a look round the ward & attended to the
patients until we arrived in Etaples at about 8.15.
Unloading took till about 9.45 pm. fried some bread for
supper & got down to it at about 10.55 pm. After leaving
that we were going out to Amiens at 11.00 pm.

Friday July 14th Vickersmont

Was called at about 4.00 am. Just outside Vickersmont
told to get ready for patients & got up & put my trousers
on & lay down again.

146

We drew into Vickersmont but did not get put onto the HP siding. So went to sleep again & slept till about 7.00 am. had wash & brush up & went for breakfast fried cheese, bread, butter, jam & tea.

Came back to coach & cleaned outside brasses & washed out the corridor Went & fetched water & came back & messed about till dinner time. Dinner bully beef, pickles, potatoes & bread. Lay down & had a short sleep, after dinner & started loading up at about 2.30 pm. Took on a good load about 796 ? coach 83 patients including several Leicester's the Leicester's 678 & 9 went over last night. Served up the teas & then washed up & afterwards sat down & wrote diary sat for a few more minutes & then got some Cocoa & served it out between us. Washed up again & got patients comfortable, the got some hot milk & fried bread for supper. Had a lay down for a bit & got to Rouen at about 2.30 am.

Saturday 15th July

Started unloading & got finished about first ? then found out some blankets for the change & went round & helped Cpl Noble gather up dirty blankets & fetch the clean ones from the stores. Finished at about 4.40 am. & got down to it at about 4.45 am. Slept on until I was wakened at 9.45 am. When we were on the run going up to Romescamps for which place we had started at about 5.20 am. Got up & had a wash etc. started folding up the blankets until the train stopped at about 10.00 am. Then I went for breakfast which consisted of fried bacon, bread, & tea. Got back to coach when train stopped again & finished folding blankets & then scrubbed out the bunks all down the coach.

Landed at Romescamp at about 12.00 noon but didn't finish the floors until about 12.30 pm. Had a wash & went for dinner but as it was langoustine so didn't bother but went to the canteen & got a tea, packet biscuits. Back to train & had a lay down& read about 20 mins & then the train started off again. Washed out passage & lay down again till tea time. Went & had bread, butter, jelly & tea & a piece of cake from Hugh ?.

Got back to the coach when the train stopped & messed about until we reached Vickersmont at about 4.45 pm. Started loading up again at about 5.15 or 5.30 & took on 300 laying cases M coach got 28 some badly knocked about.

Finished loading about 7.40 pm. & took down the names etc. Served up cocoa & got washed up again. Carried on with general ward duties then on into ….

Sunday 16th July

& when I looked at my watch & found it was 1.00 am. I was rather surprised. Kept on with ward duty until about

3.30 am. Then was relieved by Stanley & slept until about 6.00 am. Served up tea & bread & butter & washed up. Arrived in Rouen about 6.45 am. & unloaded. Unloading took till about 9.15 am. Went & had breakfast of fried bacon, bread, butter & tea. Got back to coach & folded blankets etc. & swept out.

Train started off again at about 11.10 am. for Lapugnoy Had a wash & got down to it at about 11.30 am. & slept until ^.00 pm. When I woke up & found we were just entering St Rock.

Went & had tea, bread, butter, jam, dripping & tea. Got back to at Annies ??& lay down again & read until we reached Vickersmont at about 7.10 pm. Started loading up at about &.20 pm. Loaded pretty full M coach got 77 cases. Started away at about 9.45 pm. & made headway. Served up cocoa & bread & butter & washed up. Had a bit of fried bread & drop of cocoa & then took names. Arrived at Abbeville at 12.pm. midnight.

Monday 17th July

Left Abbeville at about 12.10 am. Had a cup of tea & bit of bread & dripping & lay down as much as I could until we got to Camiers

At about 2.30 am. Unloaded & was getting to bed when I was fetched out to help unload the other coach at 4.10

am. Finished unloading & got to bed at 5.0am. Was called at 9.30 am. & found we were at Abbeville. Washed etc. Billy Eacott came over for a couple of minutes before No. 29 went out, said he had fell out with E Wells & seemed pretty sorry about it. Went & had breakfast fried bacon, bread & tea.

Back to coach & got blankets folded. Fetched water took rubbish to incinerator. Cleaned outside brasses. Knocked off at 1.10 pm.

Mail served up during morning. letter from H Hutchings & one from Syd Lester & a parcel & letter from home. Lay down from knocking off work until Parade at 2.0 pm. Attended Parade in best service dress. Inspection by C.O. was recommended for a new tunic. Told we could get down to it for the afternoon but had some letters to write, so wrote Mother, Stanley, Cath, H Hutching, S Musson. Had a tin of salmon for tea. Messed about after tea & received Birthday cards from Mother & Dad, May & Stanley. & went down to the Y. M. C. A. hut for a cup of tea & some biscuits & came back to train. Train moved out from Abbeville at 8.45 pm. For Lapugnoy. Got down to it at about 8.45 pm. & lay reading for half an hour or so then went to sleep.

Tuesday 18th July Lapugnoy

Reveille 6.00am. got up 6.20 am. Parade 7.30 had a wash & brush up & breakfast about 9am. Breakfast bread butter jam cheese & tea. Back to coach & cleaned up brasses etc. till dinner time. Langoustine for dinner so didn't bother to have any. Had some chocolate cake etc; instead. Rubbed up windows after 2.00 clock. Parade & had a lay down till teatime. After tea had a wash & brush up & fetched water then went out. Back again for 8.30 pm. Parade & then went out again to try & get some chips or potatoes. Could not get either, so came back about 9.15 pm.& had a bit of cake with Goodwin. Stopped talking to Goodwin & Brookhouse until about 10.00 pm. Then went & got down to it.

Wednesday July 19th 1916 Reveille 6.00am. Parade 6.30 am. Wash & brush up & had breakfast. Started loading at Lapugnoy at about 7.30 am. Took on about 30 patients of whom H M coach got one. Left Lapugnoy at just after 9.30 am. Next stop Chocques . Took some more patients in here & M coach got 4 more. Just about finished loading when a German Aeroplane came over & dropped a couple of bombs, the second one dropping about 50 or 60 yards away from the end of the train,

That seemed to put the wind up the driver & he started off quick. Went on to St Venant where we got a few more patients on board but M coach didn't get any this time. From St Venant we went to Melville & there took on a few more cases M coach getting another twelve, but the train was not much more than half full & this was our last call. Got away from Melville pretty early & went down to Boulogne where we arrived ???? nearly as I know at about 6.30 pm. Unloaded & got the blankets folded . Practically all the patients this trip were sick cases & the trip was quite a joy ride.

Left Boulogne at about 9.00pm.for Lapugnoy again. Had a cup of cocoa & had that & some bread & cheese for supper & got down to it soon after ten o clock.

Thursday 20th July

Was awakened this morning & found we had arrived at Lapugnoy Went on the 6.30am. Parade came back & had a wash & brush up & went & got breakfast, Bread, cheese &tea & then up came a little bit of ham on a bone & there was a raid on it.

Being only second I came off pretty well in the attack. Went & cleaned up panels & brasses until dinner time.

? Pay ? at 11.45 am. Then dinner. Heard that we were moving any minute. Had dinner, jolly good. Dinner today Roast Beef, onions, beans, potatoes, & bread followed by rice & currants after dinner were issued with ward shoes & we started out somewhere about two o'clock. Started loading up at Lille's. Took on a lot of sitting patients here of whom M coach got 76 ? men ?

From Lille went onto Ferville & took on stretcher cases 11 in M coach, making total for journey in coach 87. Served up tea, to the sitting patients & started back for Melville, for Boulogne & unloaded. Finished unloading soon after 1.00am. & got down to it at 1.30 am.

Friday 21st July

Was called at about 7.30 am. Got up & went & had breakfast fried bacon, bread, tea. Found that we were on our way back to Lapugnoy but were going back via Dunkirk, Bavelle, Hazebeuck, Berguethe, Lille, Chocques So into Lapugnoy. .Some very nice country round this route. Near Dunkirk it was very flat but very pretty. On the way round got the blankets folded & the place washed out. Arrived Lap??? At about 11.30 am. & then cleaned up the outside brasses. Went for dinner soon after 10pm.Bully beef, beans, potatoes& bread.

Backs ???messed about until 2.0 o clock. Parade then back & had a lay down for the afternoon. Tea 4.00pm. bread butter am & tea. After tea had a wash & brush up & went out, found Brookhouse & Goodwin but met Godfrey, so went with him. Came back to train soon after seven o clock & called at F coach. Goodwin was un but not Brookhouse. Sat talking for a while until Brookhouse came in at about 7.45 pm. Then went out to see about some eggs & chips for supper, ordered supper & came back to answer names on 8.30 pm. Roll Call.

Went out again & got a plate of chips and a couple of eggs & coffee for super back to train at about 9.15 pm. Sat talking to Goodwin & Brookhouse for a bit then got down to it.

Saturday 22nd July

Reveille 6.00am. Got up about 6.20am. Parade 6.30am. Breakfast 7.00am. Had a couple of poached eggs bread & butter. Started loading from 186 CJ Lag??? At 7.30am. Took on about 50 patients but none in M coach, moved out at about 8.30 am. For Lille, here we picked up more patients 12 uppers coming into M coach from Lille. We moved round to Melville. Very few patients here. M coach only got 2 more, making 14 in all. Finished picking up patients here made for Boulogne. Served up dinner 7 tea during journey, arrived in Boulogne at about 5.30 pm. Unloaded & started cleaning up.

Received letters from Mother, May & Bert & Echoers

Left Boulogne for Lap????? Again at about 8.15pm. Finished clearing up blankets & washed out coach then had some fried bread & some cocoa made with milk for supper. Got down to it soon after 10.pm.

Sunday 23rd July Lapugnoy

Woke up this morning at Lapunroy again. Parade
6.30am. felt very tired and a lay down for half an hour
after parade. Breakfast, ham, bread, & tea. After
breakfast cleaned up brasses inside and out, took till
dinner time, (or nearly) over it then sat about until dinner-
time. Heard there was to be a cricket match with 18
C.C.S. (Casualty Clearing Station.) if possible this
afternoon. Had bully beef pickles & bread. After dinner
found we could not play 18 C.C.S so arranged a match
with No. 10 Ambulance Train. Parade 2.00pm. Went over
& scored for No. 6. Result 54 runs to 42 in favour of no.
6. Back for tea but felt pretty rotten so only had a cup of
tea. After tea wrote a letter home and one to Cath. (Len's
Sweetheart.)

Still felt rotten so lay down again but went out soon after
for about three quarters of an hour. Came back and
attended 8.30pm. parade. Then came in and took
10grms of aspirin & got down to it.

Monday 24th July

Lapugvory Got up at about 6.20am. Feeling absolutely
rotten, went on Parade and came and got down for
another half hour. Felt no better so went and got a cup of

tea, couldn't eat anything fetched some water and then got on with brasses. Took all morning on the brasses and then went and got some dinner very good dinner today, Roast beef new potatoes cabbage & suet pudding. After dinner still felt pretty rotten but not quite as bad as during the morning so lay down till 2.O' clock parade. After parade was supposed to come back & work until 3.o pm. But thought it was easier to lay down so lay down till 3,0pm. Then went & scored for the cricket match which had been arranged between two teams off of the train, one side scored 82 & the other 41. Came & had tea & then still feeling rotten lay down once again, but went out for a bit soon after & got back in time for parade at 8.30pm. Came into bunk took 10 grams aspirin & got down to it.

The train moved into the hospital siding ready for loading up again.

Tuesday 25th July Lapugnoy France.

Reveille 6.00am.

Got up in time for parade, wash and brush up, went for breakfast, breakfast not ready so had to come back & help with loading which we started at about half past seven. Didn't take many cases on board & when we had finished I went & got my breakfast. No cases for M coach from Lapugnoy this trip. From Lapugnoy we took up the run at about 8.30pm & proceeded to Bethune, here we took on just a few more & again loaded a few more places ? At this stop 12 lying cases were put into M coach, but none very bad. They were mostly sick & so needed but little attention. Away once more & proceeded to Lille, here there were very few cases M coach being lucky again, we once more received no cases, from Lille we moved on once more to Melville & during this portion of the journey served up dinner to the patients & got the things washed up & cleared away. At Melville we were again only given a very few patients & M coach received but an odd one, here I went in & got my own dinner which today consisted of Roast beef & potatoes & bread. Before resuming the journey I found that from Melville we were to proceed straight down to Boulogne, leaving Merville a few minutes later we proceeded at a terribly slow pace to Hazebrouke, the line being blocked all the way. Arriving at Hazebrouke at just on 4 0 Clock. I went to the kitchen in order to draw the patients' tea but the train started off before I could get it (the tea) I rode as far as St Omer in the kitchen & got my own tea en route. On reaching St Omer of course I returned to the coach & helped to serve up the patients' tea & then Stanley proceeded down to the kitchen for his tea. Whilst I washed up the tea things & got tided up again. From Hazebrouck we made a very good rundown to Boulogne having practically only two stops on the way. St Omer & Calais, arriving in Boulogne at about 20 minutes past seven. Here we unloaded, we had on board only about

250 or 260 cases mostly sick & found we were due out again at 9.43pm. that did not leave much time & I felt too tired to clean up so after reading my letter, one from Cath one from Syd Musson & a paper from home. (newspaper I would imagine.)   I went & had a talk with French & then came back just before we moved out to make some cocoa with the milk that was left over. This we made going back up the line & both Stanley Edwards (Manchester) & self-had some bread & cheese & cocoa, didn't feel very grand all day & got down to it at about eleven or just after & slept middling.

Wednesday 26th July Lapugnoy.

Train at a standstill in the garage at Lapugnoy when I was knocked up this morning. Turned out on first parade but came back & had another half hour or so in ? again. However I thought it would be as well to go & get some breakfast so went & had some fried cheese (quite a long time since I had fried cheese) & bread & butter & tea. Came back to M coach & got on steadily with the inside brasses, went & drew a new tunic, did a good bit of messing about scrubbed the bread tray did a lot more of nothing then suddenly thought I would patch my old trousers, no sooner said or thought then started on. Managed to fire/or find a nice looking bullseye in the seat then went had dinner of Roast beef (roasted to Army Pattern) pudding(hush not a word this pudding was made of flour & water, baked in the oven with a little fat over it) & mashed potatoes I had bread (army pattern again). After dinner I did the usual i.e. lay down until the 2.00 O'clock parade. I don't expect we are supposed to do this every day but "ah our." Attended the 2 o clock parade & came back to the coach, ostensibly to work until 3.0 pm. When there was a cricket match arranged with the rails head staff. I say ostensibly because if I am to be strictly truthful I suppose I must say that I did nothing but clean about half a dozen windows ---------& lay down--------- again! At just about 3.0pm. the rail head staff discovered that they were too busy to play the match & so one was arranged between Nos 1 & 2 section of the train. Perhaps the less said about this match the better as No 2 section with 9 men when fielding & only 8 when batting, won the game by 56 runs to 44. After seeing this "brilliant Victory" we returned for tea, Bread & butter jam & tea. After tea not having any money & feeling too idle to do anything else I wrote up this little note book. (and Leonard Folwell we are so glad you did!)   Messed about generally until parade & then got down to it. My eyes were terribly bad all day.

Thursday 27th July Lapugnoy

Got up in time to go on first parade but came back & had another half an hour to rest my eyes a bit more. Had bacon & bread & tea for breakfast & came back &

cleaned some brasses. When Mr Cunningham came round (Dr) he tested my heart & said there was no trouble there. Told me to res

t as much as I could & also to rest my eyes. Having nothing else to do I rested until dinner time, then went & had my dinner, came back & rested until parade. Rested again till tea time & after tea had a rest. During the afternoon there was a football mtch between the train & 18 CCS (Casualty Clearing Station) the CCS winning by 3 goals to 2. I didn't go to that, from about 7 to 8 pm. I sat in the lounge talking to Cunningham & French found that we were going out in the morning, the train moved into the hospital siding ready, before half past eight parade. After parade took a No 9? & got down to it & knew all about the 9 during the night. (I'm not sure what 9 was possibly a tablet/drug to help him feel better.)

Friday 28th July Lapugnoy

Got up in time to miss parade this morning so went in for breakfast ; only cheese, so had a cup of tea & came out again. Started loading up at Lapugnoy took a good number of patients 12 lying coming into M coach leaving Lapugnoy at about 8.30 we proceeded to Bethune where we had to wait a good while before the patients turned up. There were a few more at any rate than last time we called but then we are taking two days loads today as there was no train around yesterday. Left Bethune & went round to Chocques where we took on more patients. From Chocques to Merville, where we filled up M coach had 42 cases altogether 22 lying & 20 sitting. Left Merville & had a pretty fair run down to Boulogne. Arrived Boulogne about 7.15pm. Mails came up & I got several letters. Terribly slow unloading. Didn't start on M coach until 9.0pm. After unloading had some bread & cheese & milk & got down to it.

Saturday 29th July Lapugnoy.

At Lapugnoy again when I woke up this morning. Went on parade & then went & got breakfast. Came back, folded up the blankets cleaned up as much of coach as possible till dinner time. Had dinner & then lay down again until 2.0pm. parade. Lay down again till 3.0pm when there was a cricket match against the Rail Head Staff, Rotten match & 6 lost only 27 to 22 being the result. Back to train & had tea, After tea went out in Lapugnoy until soon after 8.0pm then came back, attended parade & went out again for some eggs arriving back on train at about 9.20pm. Got in & got down to it.

Sunday 30th July Lapugnoy.

Got up & went on parade & had breakfast. After breakfast went & cleaned up in the coach till dinner time. Very good dinner Roast Beef, Roast Potatoes & spring cabbage. Lay down till 2.0 clock parade. At 2.30pm a cricket match against No 10. No 6 again lost by 47 to 20. After match ha tea then wrote letters until parade time. Went on parade then came in & got down to it. Train moved over into HP (Hospital) siding ready for moving in the morning.

Monday 31st July Lapugnoy.

Got up & attended parade & got back & had breakfast. Started loading up at about 7.30am. & took a good few cases. M coach getting 12 lying. Left Lapugoy about 8.40am. & went to Bethune. Here a lot more cases awaited us. M coach got more here. Bethune to Chocques where we nearly filled up.

M coach took on 15 lying making 27 in all, the full capacity . Choegues to Merville where we got about another 80 ---100 patients one sitting being put in M coach. From Mervillel a pretty decent run to Boulogne where we arrived at about 7.00pm.

In Leonard Folwell's 1916 WW1 Diary there is a list of his letters sent to home with the name of the recipient.

EG; May & Bert (Len's sister & brother-in-law.) 1/1/16

Wilf Geary 1/1/16

Aunt Amelia 1/1/16

There are also lists of French Towns with numbers and dates of where his Ambulance Train would have travelled. I have copied the names of the French Towns/Villages as they seem to be written.

Leonard received two Medals from WW1. They have ribbons but no pin marks he never wore them with pride as we felt he should.

There is a very faint list of dates with how much he had been paid.

January – paid   17/.0 (Shillings) Drawn .3.7 credit 13/5
.

Feb.   -------- paid £1.9.0 Drawn 19.1   credit 9.11

March --------paid   £1.11.0 Drawn 19.11 credit 13.1

April -----------paid 19./6   Drawn 14/.4 credit 5,/2

May ------------paid 15,/6   Drawn 1.2.0   credit 6.6

June-------------paid 15./0   Drawn 14.0   credit   1.0

July ------------paid   15/.6   Drawn 15./9   credit ---3

August --------paid 15./6   Drawn 17./11   credit 2.5

Sept ----------paid 15./0   Drawn 17./11   credit
£1.13.5 –2.5

Oct   ----------paid15.6

Also in the Diary are Cricket Scores and a list of friends
and family and the dates he wrote to them.

 NB During March you will notice there is not a lot of
content in this diary, we presume this is when he was
spending time at the local hospitals training for his life
and work on Ambulance Train No. six.

This diary has been painstakingly copied by hand into an
exercise book, where it was then copied onto the
computer for safe keeping. Several times I forgot to save
it and many times lost part of it or all of it.

It has been a labour of Love and I'm so relieved and
happy that at long last we have a copy of this unique
"Little Black Book!" A diary from WW1 1916. I hope all of
you who read this diary will get as much information and
inspiration from it as I have coping it.

We are not sure of the date that Leonard joined the army
but we know he left Aldershot and headed for
Southampton on 20th January 1916. We also know that

he worked on ambulance train number six, this was a French train and the French trains were not as well equipped as the later British trains.

His diary is not clear on what he did in the first two to three months when he was first in France. Reading between the lines I have told how I feel he went to the local field hospitals to learn first aid and how to look after the injured men.

We know he was out in France during The Battle of The Somme, as on Friday 14th July his Diary states: 'Vickersmont. Took on a good load about 796 including several Leicester's, the Leicester's 678 & 9 went over last night and we have several of the Leicester's on our train today.' He never mentioned The Battle of the Somme.

I hope you have enjoyed my story about Leonard's War. I hope it has given you an insight of what Len's life could have been like.

I realise that the Ambulance Trains would have been so busy and packed that the orderlies would not have had the time or room to visit and treat patients individually.

My Grandfather Leonard Folwell died after a short illness in 1981, aged 85.

When the hospital gave my mother his clothes and belongings, they said, 'He didn't have any money on him.' When my mother arrived home and went through his things she found £20.00 in his wallet that he had sewn into the back of his belt.

INSIDE OF LEONARD'S DIARY

LEONARD'S MEDALS

Chapter Twenty Two

<u>THE UNKNOWN WARRIOR</u>

On 7th November 1920, in strictest secrecy, four unidentified British bodies were exhumed from temporary battlefield cemeteries at Ypres, Arras, the Aisne and the Somme.

 None of the soldiers who did the digging were told why.

The bodies were taken by field ambulance to GHQ (Government Head Quarters.) at Saint-Pol-sur-Ternoise. Once there the bodies were draped with the union flag.

One body was chosen and placed in a wooden coffin. The coffin bore the inscription:

A British Warrior who fell in the Great War 1914-1918 for King and Country.

The other three bodies were reburied

The railway carriage which brought the body to London has been restored and can be viewed at Bodiam station, Sussex, where a replica of the coffin is on display.

The Burial

On the morning of 11th November the coffin was placed, by the bearer party from the 3rd Battalion Coldstream Guards, on a gun carriage drawn by six black horses of the Royal Horses Artillery. It then began its journey through the crowd-lined streets, making its first stop in Whitehall where the Cenotaph was unveiled by King George V. the King placed his wreath of red roses and bay leaves on the coffin. His card read:

"In proud memory of those Warriors who died unknown in the Great War. Unknown, and yet well known: as dying, and behold they live. George R.I. 11th November 1920."

The entourage then made its way to the north door of Westminster Abbey.

The coffin was borne to the west end of the nave through a congregation of around 1,000 mourners and a guard of honour of 100 holders of the Victory Cross.

While the choir sang the 23rd Psalm, The Lord's My Shepherd.

After the hymn 'Lead Kindly Light ' the King stepped forward and dropped a handful of French earth onto the coffin from a silver shell as it was lowered into the grave.

At the close of the service the hymn "Abide with Me" was sung, after which the Reveille was sounded.

Servicemen kept watch at each corner of the grave while thousands of mourners file past.

The grave was filled in using 100 sandbags of earth from the battlefields, on the 18th November.

On 11th November 1921 the present black marble stone was unveiled at a special service.

The inscription on the stone reads.

BEANEATH THIS STONE REST THE BODY

OF A BRITISH WARRIOR

UNKNOWN BY NAME OR RANK

BROUGHT FROM FRANCE TO LIE AMONG

THE MOST ILLUSTRIOUS OF THE LAND

AND BURIED HERE ON ARMISTICE DAY

11TH NOV: 1920, IN THE PRESENCE OF

HIS MAJESTY KING GEORGE V

HIS MINISTERS OF STATE

THE CHIEFS OF HIS FORCES

AND A VAST CONCOURSE OF THE NATION

THUS ARE COMMEMORATED THE MANY

MULITUDES WHO DURING THE GREAT

WAR OF 1914-1918 GAVE THE MOST THAT

MAN CAN GIVE LIFE ITSELF

FOR GOD

FOR KING AND COUNTRY

FOR LOVED ONES HOME AND EMPIRE

FOR THE SACRED CAUSE OF JUSTICE AND

THE FREEDOM OF THE WORLD

THEY BURIED HIM AMONG THE KINGS BECAUSE

HE HAD DONE GOOD TOWARDS GOD AND

TOWARD HIS HOUSE.

Around the main inscription are four texts:

(top) THE LORD KNOWETH THEM THAT ARE HIS.

(sides) GREATER LOVE HATH NO MAN THAN THIS

UNKNOWN AND YET WELL KNOWN, DYING AND
BEHOLD WE LIVE,

(base) IN CHRIST SHALL ALL BE MADE ALIVE

When the Duke of York (later King George VI) married
Lady Elizabeth Bowes Lyons (who later became The

Queen Mother) in the Abbey in 1923 she laid her wedding bouquet on the grave as a mark of respect (she had lost her brother during the war.)

All royal brides married in the Abbey since then have sent back their bouquets to be laid on the grave.

The Unknown Warrior became a symbol for families who had lost loved ones.

OUR FALLEN HEROES

Scattered across the French Countryside
Row upon row of white grave stones.
In memory of the fallen. A century ago
Fathers, Sons, Husbands, Lovers
Lying where they fell.

Across our land in many churches
Stands a wooden cross
That once stood on the fields of Flanders
A reminder of a local soldier.
A much loved Son, Brother, Husband

In London inside the Great West Door of Westminster Abbey
For all to see
A lone grave of an unknown Warrior
A reminder of the sacrifice made.

Our service men and women
Still give their lives for us today
So we can live in Peace and Harmony.
They return home from the conflict with missing limbs and broken minds
so hard to heal.
Let us find them a place of sanctuary.

WW1 Royal Army Medical Corps Postcard

Printed in Poland
by Amazon Fulfillment
Poland Sp. z o.o., Wrocław